AF538534

Chanakya Neeti

Chanakya Neeti

R.P. Jain

Published by
Ocean Books (P) Ltd.
4/19 Asaf Ali Road,
New Delhi-110 002 (INDIA)
e-mail: info@oceanbooks.in

ISBN 978-81-8430-211-0
CHANAKYA NEETI
by Shri R.P. Jain

Edition
2025

Price
₹ 400.00 (Rupees Four Hundred only)

Printed at
Narula Printers, Delhi

PREFACE

Vishnugupt Chanakya was unlike other children, an extraordinary child. His father Chanakya was a teacher. He also wanted to become a teacher like his father. He studied politics and economics from Takshashila University. He had already studied the 'Vedas' (Hindu sacred scriptures), 'Puranas' (Hindu mythology), etc. in his youth itself. His *Chanakya Neeti* is an extract from the 'Vedic scriptures'.

All through his learning, his teachers were impressed by his sharp intellect and reasoning power; he was appropriately called 'Kautilya' (master of astuteness). After completing his education, he started teaching in Takshashila University itself. Having studied politics, he kept a close watch over national and international political happenings from the beginning. During this period, he closely tracked the invaders of Northern India like Seleucus and Sikander (Alexander). Even in his home and neighbouring States, the state of affairs were not normal. The subjects were unjustly and heavily taxed by the rulers. They were intolerably burdened. All these circumstances disturbed Chanakya. He also wanted India to be united. He, therefore, took a vow to serve the nation. He left the teaching job at Takshashila University and came to Patliputra.

In Patliputra, when he met King Ghananand, he bluntly told him of his shortcomings and the hardships being faced by the masses. King Ghananand, who was used to appeasement, could not tolerate such bluntness. Even though Chanakya was exceptionally intelligent, he was ugly looking; he also did not like his looks and he expelled him from his palace. In turn, Chanakya pledged to wipe out the Nand race, which he successfully achieved with the help of Chandragupt.

Chanakya had a tough life; it was filled with all kinds of difficulties and irrelevance. He had to fight it out at every step to move ahead. Some people may think that his lifes view kindled the spirit of vengeance or retaliation. But his retaliation was not for personal reasons but on account of his concern for the masses. He had seen their sufferings and pains, even felt it. He had appealed to King Ghananand on their behalf. Since King Ghananand was not a well-wisher of his subjects, Chanakya pledged to destroy him.

Chanakya worked for Chadragupt and then for his son, Bindusaar as their minister and special advisor. But it was tragic that he was deceitfully killed by Subandhu, a minister of Bindusaar.

He left behind *Chanakya Neeti*, a treasure trove for the world. This treasure is being dedicated to you, the reader. It is hoped that you will benefit from it.

—Mahesh Sharma

CONTENTS

BRIEF BIOGRAPHY OF ACHARYA CHANAKYA

Chanakya is known in India as a great politician and economist. His father Chanak 'Muni' (Hermit) was a great teacher. It is believed that Chanakya was born in Takshashila or in Southern India, in the year 350 B.C. He died around 283 B.C.

Chanakya is also known as Vishnugupt, Vatsyayan, Mallnaag, Pakshil Swami, Angal, Dramil and Kautilya. Child is the father of man. This saying applies to Chanakya hundred per cent. Consider the following events:

- Chanakya was born with a complete set of teeth, a sign that he would become king or emperor. Since he was born in a Brahmin family, this wouldn't have been possible, so his teeth were broken. However, it was prophesied that he would be a king-maker and rule through him.
- From childhood, Chanakya possessed leadership traits. He was much more intelligent and understanding, for his age.
- Chanakya was very blunt. For this reason, he was expelled by King Ghananand of Patliputra from his court. Then, Chanakya had pledged to wipe out the Nand race.
- To achieve his intent, he chose the young Chandragupt, whom he felt had all the qualities to become a king.
- Chandragupt had several enemies. King Ghananand was one of them, who had tried to kill him by poisoning him, several times. To enhance Chandragupt's immunity against poison,

Chanakya had purposely started mixing small doses of poison, in his food.

- Chandragupt was unaware of this. So, one day he shared his food with his wife, who, at that time, was nine months' pregnant. She could not tolerate it and she expired. However, the child was saved by Chanakya, by splitting her womb.
- This child grew up to become Emperor Bindusaar. He had a minister called Subandhu. Subandhu could not tolerate Chanakya. So, he repeatedly badgered King Bindusaar that Chanakya is the killer of his mother.
- Bindusaar believed it without verifying the facts and offended Chanakya. However, when he came to know the truth, he felt ashamed and apologised to Chanakya. He also ordered Subandhu to apologise to Chanakya.
- Subandhu was a very devious person. In the guise of seeking his apology, he killed Chanakya by deceit. A political conspiracy brought about the end of a great personality.

Education

Chanakya's father was a teacher. So he fully understood the importance of education. He provided the best education to his son. When most children would learn to speak, Chanakya had already started learning the Vedas. At a very young age, Chanakya mastered the Vedas and developed interest for politics. Soon he started understanding the finer points of politics. He learnt how to plant operatives in the enemy camp and the art of spying. Apart from this, he studied economics and the Hindu scriptures in depth. Later, he wrote the eternally applicable, great manuscripts like *Chanakya Neeti*, *Neetishastra* and *Arthashastra*.

Takshashila (now in Pakistan) was one of the top universities in India, where Chanakya gained practical and applied knowledge in different subjects. The students were taught science, ayurveda treatment, philosophy, grammar, mathematics, economics, astrology, history, astronomy, agricultural science and medicine science. The teachers there were exceptional scholars in their subjects. His popularity during his student days can be gauged from the fact that he was also called 'Kautilya' and 'Vishnugupt' by the people.

After finishing his education in Takshashila, Chanakya started teaching there. He was the students' model. They were prepared to do anything on his command. Two of his students—Bhadrabhatt and Purushdutt were very close to him. It has been said that they played a vital role in helping him to attain his mission and even that they spied for him.

During this period, Chanakya learned from his sources that a great emperor of Greece, Seleucus, was about to attack the weak rulers of India. The unity of India was in danger. Taking advantage of the anarchical situation, Patliputra's cruel ruler Ghananand started exploiting his subjects. On the pretext of defending against the threat of foreign invasion, he imposed several new taxes on the people. While on the one hand, there was threat of attack from the foreign rulers, on the weak States; on the other hand, even their neighbouring States were preparing to invade such weak States. Chanakya was keeping a close watch on both the dangers. All these likely upheavals were giving him sleepless nights. He decided to move from Takshashila to Patliputra.

In Patliputra

Patliputra's (now Patna) history has been much checkered. Like Delhi, it was built and destroyed, several times. China's famous traveler, Fa-Xian had visited Patliputra in 399 B.C. and had said that it was a prosperous city, rich in natural resources. During the same period, another Chinese traveler, Huen-Tsang had described it as a destructed city. Shishudhavanshi had established this city on the southern bank of the Ganges river. Over the time, it has been renamed several times—Pushpur, Pushpnagar, Kusumpur, Patliputra and now it is called Patna.

When Chanakya reached here, it was known as a place which respected its scholars and intelligentsia. Scholars from all over the country were invited respectfully for giving new ideas and suggesting ways for the improvement of the State. So, Chanakya decided to initiate his mission to unite the country from here.

Chanakya's Pledge

King Ghananand of Patliputra was an irresponsible, selfish and cruel person. His only aim was to anyhow amass wealth. His greed for wealth was insatiable inspite of the fact that he had hoarded huge wealth. His subjects hated him but no one dared to raise his voice. His subjects were intolerably burdened with several types of taxes. Even leather, wood and stones were taxed.

When Chanakya reached Patliputra, King Ghananand's stance had softened a bit. He set up a committee to help the poor. The committee consisted of scholars and influential persons of the society.

Since Chanakya was a great scholar of Takshashila, he was also included in the committee. Later, Chanakya was made the head of this committee which was named as 'Sungha'. The head of the committee was required to meet the king regularly. After becoming the head, when Chanakya met King Ghananand for the first time, he was humiliated by him for his ugly looks. He also could not tolerate Chanakya's bitter but true words. Over the time Ghananand's hatred for Chanakya grew. Their enmity kept growing. Chanakya did not believe in appeasement and used to work professionally. He used to put across his views briefly but frankly. The king thoroughly disliked Chanakya's attitude. So, one day he removed him from his post and expelled him from his palace. This insult infuriated Chanakya and he pledged that he would not knot his hair called '*choti*' till he deposed Ghananand from his throne.

Meeting with Chandragupt

After being humiliated, Chanakya rushed out of the palace onto the streets of Patliputra like a wild bull. He was pricked by a thorn, he stumbled but balanced himself. The scholar Chanakya had his own peculiar ways to deal with situations. He looked at the thorny plant. He was furious at that moment and he did want his anger to disorient him. So, he calmly sat down in the blazing sun and started to uproot the plant. After a while, after successfully uprooting the plant, he threw it aside and continued on his way. When he was uprooting the thorny plant, his absorption was being watched by a youth. He was Chandragupt, the future ruler of the Maurya Empire. His face had a dazzling glow. He was impressed by Chanakya's determination and he wanted to talk to the scholar.

He walked up to him and spoke to him respectfully. Chanakya asked him about his family background, "Who are you? You seem disturbed?"

The young Chandragupt bowing respectfully said, "Sir, your opinion is correct. I am in great difficulty. But I do not wish to bother you with my troubles".

Chanakya said sympathetically, "You may share your troubles with me without any hesitation. If it is in my power, I will help you".

"I am the grandson of King Sarwarthsidhi. He had two queens—Sunanda Devi and Mura Devi. Sunanda had nine sons, who were called Navnands. Mura had one son, my father. The Navnands tried to kill my father repeatedly. We were more than one hundred brothers. The Navnands were determined to kill us out of jealousy. I have somehow survived; but my life is ruined. I want to take revenge from Nand, who is now the ruler."

Enemy's enemy is a friend. The hurt Chanakya got a friend, who was also against Nand. Chandragupt's story shocked Chanakya. He became emotional and pledged that he will not rest till he destroys Nand and reposes Chandragupt to his rightful place, on the throne of Patliputra.

Chanakya said, "I shall get you the throne of Patliputra, Chadragupt". From that day, Chandragupt and Chanakya became occupied in ending the misrule of the cruel and despotic Nand.

Not much information has been documented on Chandragupt, his birth place, his family background and other events of his life. There are different versions in different manuscripts about his parents. In fact, it may be true that he was related to the Maurya dynasty. Possibly, that is why, he was called 'Chandragupt Maurya'. It is also said that his mother was the daughter of a village head. His father was the king of a wild forest called Pipatvan and was killed during a war. Thereafter, he came to Patliputra with his mother.

Chandragupt had leadership qualities by birth. Even children used to consider him as their leader. He used to hold his court as the children's king and delivered justice. His traits of courage and understanding were apparent from his childhood. When Chanakya was passing through the streets of Patliputra, he had seen Chandragupt seated on a throne like high rock, in a royal style. A group of children was seeking justice from him. He was very much impressed by Chandragupt's imposing looks and intelligent dialogue.

Chandragupt studied for the next seven to eight years. His teachers were selected by Chanakya. Thereafter, he became expert in the art of fighting and administration.

Sikander's Attack

During this period, Chandragupt's and Chanakya's friendship bond became stronger. They formed a large army to counter the enemies. They also witnessed several historic events. As Chandragupt's training had been completed, Chanakya gave him a free hand to test his fighting abilities. A simple village boy had now become a powerful army commander. Chandragupt and his army got strength from Chanakya's brain and great personality.

For tens of years, Sikander and other invaders had attacked the Indian continent. Chanakya had studied Sikander's war strategies in depth. He was also conscious of the Indian ruler's weaknesses.

It is said that Chandragupt and Sikander also fought each other. Chandragupt's arrogance and hard attitude angered Sikander. He captured Chandragupt.

Sikander's power had started waning due to the depletion of his commanders. First, a brave commander named Nikosar was killed. Then another commander named Philip, who was considered invincible, was killed. His death shook up Sikander. After Sikander's death in Babylonia, all his commanders were either killed or driven away. In 321 B.C., all his officers divided his empire amongst themselves. It also ended their rule over the area east of Sindhu River.

Nand's Defeat

Before attacking Nand, Chanakya prepared a strong war strategy. He first tried this strategy by attacking the centre of the state. But they repeatedly faced defeat. Chandragupt and Chanakya then changed their war strategy and attacked the borders of the Magadha Empire. They were again disappointed.

Chandragupt and Chanakya then revamped their war strategy, taking lesson from their past mistakes. They befriended

King Parvartak (or Porus the second). Consequently, Parvartak, his brother, Verochak and son, Mallayaketu joined them with their armies. King Nand also had the support of a large army. His able minister, Amatya Rakshas was loyal to him and was no less than a boon for him. Chanakya prepared a plan and planted his spies in Nands camp. In a short period, he learnt their shortcomings. Nand and Amatya Rakshas were also planning to counter Chanakya's attack.

The details of the war between Nand and Chandragupt are not available. But most certainly it must have been fierce and frightful battle. Nand, his sons and other relations were all killed. Amatya Rakshas became helpless. Thus, Chanakya destroyed the Nand race.

Chanakya's Principal Concern

Chanakya's life was full of vengeances; it inspires people to be revengeful. But personal vengeance was not Chanakya's intention. He wanted that the State was protected, it was ruled systematically and its subjects lived happily-peacefully. To ensure the prosperity of the people, he did two things. First, he appointed Amatya Rakshas as Chandragupt's minister; second, a book was written, which detailed the code of conduct for the king, on how he should protect himself and his people, from enemy attack; on how to ensure the maintenance of law and order.

Chanakya's dream was that India should lead the world politically, economically and socially. His book *Arthashashtra* depicts India of his dreams. In his *Neetisashtra* and *Chanakya Neeti*, his sharp thoughts are a motivation. Some of his ideas portray his social point of view:

- In the common man's affluence and happiness is the affluence and happiness of the king. In their welfare is the kings welfare. The king should not think about his self-interest and welfare but seek happiness, in his subjects happiness.

- The king's mission should be to constantly make efforts for the welfare of his subjects. It is his duty to maintain orderly administration. His greatest reward is to treat everyone uniformly.
- Self-dependent economy is the best economy; it should not be entirely dependent on exports.
- Everyone in the society should be equal with equal opportunities.
- According to Chanakya, it is necessary to have an effective land management policy, for the development of the resources. The administration should also keep a close watch on the landlords so that they do not grab excessive land and misuse it.
- The State should keep a constant watch on the agricultural development. The State administration should constantly work towards upgrading all the steps involved from sowing of seeds to harvesting of the produce.
- The law of the land should be uniform for everyone.
- The security of its residents should be a priority for the government, as it is the sole protector, apathy towards it can jeopardise the security.

Chanakya wanted to establish a society which laid greater stress on spiritual satisfaction rather than on physical pleasures. According to him, for the development of inner strength and character, spiritual development was necessary. For the country and its society, the benefits from physical pleasures were second to the benefits from spiritual development.

The guidelines framed 2,300 years back by Chanakya are relevant even today. Even if his political principles are followed partly, then any State can become great, become a leader and set example for others.

Chapter 1

Praṇamya Śirasā Viṣṇuṃ Trailōkyādhipati Prabhum.
Nānāśāstrōddhṛtaṃ Vakṣyē Rājanītisamuccayam..

1.1 As per the Indian culture, before starting any auspicious work, prayers are offered to invoke God, for seeking his blessings. Chanakya also offered prayer to the creator of the three worlds—earth, heaven and hell; omniscient, omnipresent before starting his great manuscript. Invoking God he said, "Oh God! For the benefit of mankind, I am about to start work on these political guidelines collected from different manuscripts. So, Oh God! Please grant me strength and your blessings."

Adhītyēdaṃ Yathāśāstraṃ Narō Jānāti Sattama:.
Dharmōpadēśavikhyātaṃ Kāryākāryaṃ Śubhāśubham..

1.2 Through the study of this manuscript, after thought and reflection, even an ordinary person will gain knowledge to distinguish between capability-incompetence and right-wrong. Through this manuscript, I wish to create consciousness in human beings towards good deeds versus sins, morality versus immorality and duty versus irresponsibility. By observing this moral behaviour, human beings should enlighten their lives. Then, the purpose of this manuscript will be fulfilled.

Tadahaṃ Sampravakṣyāmi Lōkānāṃ Hitakāmyayā.
Yēna Vijñānamātrēṇa Sarvajñatvaṃ aprapadyatē..

1.3 For the benefit of the mankind, I shall describe those secret mysteries of politics, the knowledge of which will make man omniscient. If he follows the thoughts on moral behaviour in this manuscript, then most certainly, he shall attain success.

Mūrkhaśiṣyōpadēśēna Duṣṭastrībharaṇēna Ca.
Du:Khitai: Samprayōgēṇa Paṇḍitōpyavasīdati..

1.4 By preaching foolish pupils, looking after a wicked woman or keeping company of worried persons, even scholars will suffer. Therefore, foolish persons should never be encouraged to undertake any good deed. One must stay away from a characterless woman, otherwise his image will be tarnished. Similarly, an unhappy person can never give happiness, so stay away from him.

Duṣṭā Bhāryā Śaṭhaṃ Mitraṃ Bhṛtyaścōttaradāyaka:.
Sasarpē Ca Gṛhē Vāsō Mṛtyurēva Na Saṃśaya:..

1.5 A person who keeps company of a sharp-tongued woman, a sinful friend, also retains a traitorous and selfish servant, is playing with his life. Such a person can be consumed by death any time.

Āpadarthē Dhanaṃ Rakṣēd Dārān Rakṣēddanairapi.
Ātmānaṃ Satataṃ Rakṣēd Dārairapi Dhanairapi..

1.6 Any person, who saves for hard times or crisis, is an intelligent person. All efforts must be made to protect such savings. A woman is also like your wealth, so she must also be protected. But before this, he must ensure his own security, for only if he is secure he will be capable to secure his wealth and woman.

Āpadarthē Dhanaṃ Rakṣēcchrīmatāṃ Kuta Āpada:.
Kadāciccalitē Lakṣmī: Sancitōapi Vinaśyati..

1.7 People must save for crisis. But he should never think that he will be able to avert the crisis by his wealth. Lakshmi, the Goddess of wealth, is mobile; it is never permanent at any place. While accumulation of wealth is an indication of intelligence but it does not mean that crisis can be averted.

Yasmin Dēśē Na Sammānō Na Vattirna Ca Bāndhavā:.
Na Ca Vidyāgama: Kaścit Taṃ Dēśaṃ Parivarjayēt..

1.8 Any place, where man does not have respect-honour, no sources of income/employment, suitable well wishing friends/ relations, facilities for learning-education, such a place is most unsuitable. It should be left without any delay.

Dhanika: Śrōtriyō Rājā Nadī Vaidyastu Pañcama:.
Pañca Yatra Na Vidyantē Na Tatra Divasaṃ Vasēt..

1.9 Any place, which lacks the five basic conveniences, i.e. Brahmins to perform religious ceremonies, a just king, prosperous traders, flowing rivers and proper medical facilities, such a place is totally unsuitable for an intelligent person. It should be left immediately.

Lōkayātrā Bhayaṃ Lajjā Dākṣiṇyaṃ Tyāgaśīlatā.
Pañca Yatra Na Vidyantē Na Kuryāt Tatra Saṃsthitim..

1.10 In a place where the people do not have faith in this world or the next world, who do not believe in the existence of God, who do not believe in the welfare of others or in donating, an intelligent person should never consider settling there.

Jānīyāt Prēṣaṇē Bhṛtyān Bāndhavān Vyasanāgamē.
Mitraṃ Cāpattikālēṣu Bhāryāṃ Ca Vibhavakṣayē..

1.11 Servants are tested by fulfilment of their responsibilities, friends are tested in times of crisis, relations are tested in times of sorrow or incurable sickness and a woman is tested when you have no money.

Āturē Vyasanē Prāptē Durbhikṣē Śatru-Saṅkaṭē.
Rājadvārē Śmaśānē Ca Yastiṣṭhati Sa Bāndhava:..

1.12 According to Chanakya, a man's true well-wisher is the one who extends supports in sickness, famine, being bothered by an enemy, in a difficult situation or in a crisis and after death, partakes in your cremation. In other words, a true friend is the one who shares both, your happiness and sorrow.

Yō Dhruvāṇi Parityajya Adhruvaṃ Pariṣēvatē.
Dhruvāṇi Tasya Naśyanti Adhruvaṃ Naṣṭamēva Ca..

1.13 People, who stray from their planned and feasible tasks and jump to unplanned and unachievable tasks, never succeed. They should, therefore, attempt only those tasks, which they are confident of achieving.

Varayēt Kulajāṃ Prājñō Virūpāmapi Kanyakām..
Rūpavatīṃ Na Nīcasya Vivāha: Sudṛśē Kulē..

1.14 Even an ugly woman of upper caste is more suited for a scholar and an intelligent person. They should, therefore, marry an upper caste woman of equal status. Contrarily, marrying a beautiful woman of lower caste results in destruction of intellect and wisdom. Such relations are temporary and scholars should avoid them.

Nakhīnā Ca Nadīnāṃ Śṛgīṇāṃ Śastrapāṇinām.
Viśvāsō Naiva Kartavya: Strīṣu Rājakulēṣu Ca..

1.15 Sharp clawed beasts, long horned animals, rapidly flowing rivers, armed persons, women and relations of royalty are not trustworthy. In other words, they can deceive any time. People should not trust them.

Viṣādapyamṛtaṃ Grāhyamamēdhyādapi Kāñcanam.
Nīcādapyuttamā Vidyā Strīratnaṃ Duṣkulādapi..

1.16 According to Chanakya, if it is possible to extract nectar from poison, then it should be consumed without any hesitation. Similarly, you must accept gold extracted from impure metals, learning from a common man and a cultured woman from low caste without delay.

Strīṇāṃ adviguṇa Āhārō Buaddhistāsāṃ Caturguṇā.
Sāhasaṃ Ṣaḍguṇaṃ Caiva Kāmōṣṭaguṇa Ucyatē..

1.17 About women, Chanakya says that, as compared to men, their diet is twice as much, modesty is four times, courage is six times and desire for sex is eight times.

❑

Chapter 2

Anṛtaṃ Sāhasaṃ Māyā Mūrkhatvamatilubdhatā.
Aśaucatvaṃ Nidrayatvaṃ Strīṇāṃ Dōṣā: Svabhāvajā:..

2.1 According to Chanakya, natural shortcomings are personal for everyone. Everyone is born with some natural shortcomings. He has included lying, cunning, foolishness, greed, impurity and cruelty in women as natural shortcomings. But he also qualifies that it is not necessary that every woman has the above-mentioned shortcomings.

Bhōjyaṃ Bhōjanaśakitaśca Ratiśakitarvarāṅganā.
Vibhavō Dānaśakitaśca Nālpasya Tapasa: Phalam..

2.2 Chanakya says that being able to afford and eat delicacies; a woman having beauty and sexual prowess; someone having huge wealth as well as the spirit of charity, are rare virtues only obtained as a result of devotional prayer or the good deeds of the previous birth.

Yasya Putrō Vaśībhūtō Bhāryā Chandānugāminī.
Vibhavē Yaśca Santuṣṭastasya Svarga Ihaiva Hi..

2.3 Any person, whose son is obedient, wife is loyal, well-mannered and is fully satisfied with his hard-earned income, enjoys the bliss of heaven in his lifetime. In other words, he is extremely satisfied and happy.

Tē Putrā Yē Piturbhaktā: Sa Pitā Yastu Pōṣaka:.
Tanmitraṃ Yasya Viśvāsa: Sā Bhāryā Yatra Nirvṛtti:..

2.4 According to Chanakya, a true son is the one, who always obeys his parents. Only a person, who brings up his child properly, looks after his sorrow and happiness, is fit to be a father, in real terms. Only a trustworthy person can be a true friend and a woman, who delivers happiness to her husband, can, in fact, be called a wife.

Parōkṣē Kāryahantāraṃ Pratyakṣē Priyavādinam.
Varjayēt Tādṛśaṃ Mitraṃ Viṣakumbhaṃ Payōmukham..

2.5 Like most fruits which look good from outside are not sweet, similarly, people who talk sweet can be dangerous and untrustworthy. People, who flatter on your face and criticise behind your back, are not fit to be friends. They are like poison in milk. One should always be cautious of them and get rid of them at the earliest.

Na Viśvasēt Kumitrē Ca Mitrē Cāpi Na Viśvasēt.
Kadācit Kupitaṃ Mitraṃ Sarvaṃ Guahyaṃ Prakāśayēt..

2.6 Although, according to Chanakya, one should not trust a mean friend, he has suggested being wary of good and well meaning friend also. In this context, he says that in case the well meaning friend turns enemy, then because he is aware of your personal secrets, he can cause damage to you.

Manasā Cintitaṃ Kāryaṃ Vācā Naiva Prakāśayēt.
Mantrēṇa Rakṣayēd Gūḍhaṃ Kāryē Cāpi Niyōjayēt..

2.7 While planning out or implementing any desired work, if you disclose it, its successful conclusion becomes doubtful. So, take care not to disclose it to anyone till its successful conclusion.

Kaṣṭaṃ Ca Khalu Mūrkhatvaṃ Kaṣṭaṃ Ca Khalu Yauvanam.
Kaṣṭāt Kaṣṭataraṃ Caiva Paragēhanivāsanam..

2.8 Ignorance is not only painful but man is also subjected to mockery on account of it, adolescence can also cause extreme pain. But, according to Chanakya, being dependent on someone is most painful. Such a person can be compared to an animal. He has to act on someone elses orders. So, man should live life with strength.

Śailē Śailē Na Māṇikyaṃ Maukitakaṃ Na Gajē Gajē.
Sādhavō Na Hi Sarvatra Candanaṃ Na Vanē Vanē..

2.9 It is not necessary that every mountain has a precious stone's mine, every elephants forehead is adorned with the mother of pearl, every place is inhabited by gentlemen and every forest contains sandalwood trees. In other words, this world is inhabited by people of different characteristics. We must, therefore, develop contacts only with gentlemen and superior persons. This will ensure fulfilment of the desired work.

Putrāśca Vividhai: Śīlairniyōjyā: Satataṃ Budhai:.
Nītijñā: Śīlasampannā Bhavanti Kulapūjitā:..

2.10 Knowledgeable persons are able to eliminate ignorance through their knowledge, so they must build the character of their children. They must develop their talents through proper education and devotion. This will make their inbuilt talents worthy of worship and respect. Through this shloka, Chanakya, appreciating the talented person, says that like you automatically bow your head in respect when you see a religious place, similarly, talented people by becoming symbols of knowledge and belief, find a place in the hearts of people.

Mātā Śatru: Pitā Vairī Yēna Bālō Na Pāṭhita:.
Na Śōbhatē Sabhāmadhyē Haṃsamadhyē Bakō Yathā..

2.11 Foolish and ignorant people are subjected to mocking. Amongst the learned people, their condition is like that of a crow amongst swans. He is neither able to express his ideas nor is he able to accept ideas of wisdom of others. For this reason, Chanakya says that those parents, who do not arrange for proper education of their children, are their worst enemies.

Lālanād Bahavō Dōṣāstāḍanād Bahavō Guṇā:.
Tasmātputraṃ Ca Śiṣyaṃ Ca Tāḍayēnna Tu Lālayēt..

2.12 According to Chanakya, by pampering and accepting all the right or wrong demands of their children, they develop several bad habits. These bad habits hinder their progress and development in the future. It is, therefore, essential to discipline them also, in addition to loving them. A potter also needs to pat, caress and even beat the rotating mound on his wheel, to shape it into a beautiful pottery. Parents must also bring up and shape their children like the potter shapes his pottery.

Ślōkēna Vā Tadardhēna Pādēnaikākṣarēṇa Vā.
Abandhyaṃ Divasaṃ Kuryād Dānādhyayanakarmabhi:..

2.13 Life's every moment, hour and day is important. So, man must use it purposefully. For this, it is necessary that everyday he does self-study of a ved mantra, half a shloka, shlokansh or a word. If for any reason he is unable to do so, then he must donate. If it is not possible to donate, then he should perform an act of kindness or do a good deed during the day. People, who do not follow this, are wasting every moment of their life.

Kāantāviyōga: Svajanāpamāna: Ṛṇasya Śēṣaṃ Kunṛpasya Sēvā.
Daridrabhāvō Viṣamā Sabhā Ca Vināgnimētē Pradahanti Kāyam..

2.14 There are some sorrows in a man's life which are impossible to forget. Losing your wife, an insult by a near and dear one, burden of debt, serving a wicked master and living a life of poverty with fools—these hardships cause illness and push a man towards death.

Nadītīrē Ca Yē Vṛkṣā: Paragēhēṣu Kāminī.
Mantrihīnāśca Rājāna: Śīghraṃ Naśyantyasaṃśayam..

2.15 Chanakya says that as the trees on the banks of a rapidly flowing river are damaged soon, similarly a woman staying with another man or a king without an able minister is ruined soon.

Balaṃ Vidyā Ca Viprāṇāṃ Rājñāṃ Sainyaṃ Balaṃ Tathā.
Vittaṃ Ca Vaiśyānāṃ Śūdrāṇāṃ Paricaryikā..

2.16 According to Chanakya, as a Brahmin with the power of his knowledge, a king with the might of his army, a businessman with his wealth and a scheduled caste with his servility express their existence, similarly, everyman's existence is expressed by some form of power. He is completely useless without any power.

Nirdhanaṃ Puruṣaṃ Vēśyā Prajā Bhagnaṃ Nṛpaṃ Tyajēt.
Khagā Vītaphalaṃ Vṛkṣa Bhuktvā Cābhyāgatā Gṛham..

2.17 Chanakya says that a guest is important only if his stay is short. If without hesitation or shamelessly he extends his stay, then it is graceless, as a prostitute leaves a poor man, the subjects leave a defeated king and birds leave a dead tree, similarly, a guest must quickly leave after having and praising the food, offered to him.

Gṛhītvā Dakṣiṇāṃ Viprāstyajanti Yajamānakam.
Prāptavidyā Guruṃ Śiṣyā Dagdhāraṇyaṃ Mṛgāstathā..

2.18 Chanakya says that as a Brahmin moves on after receiving offerings, a student goes his way after completing his education and animals abandon a burnt forest, similarly, a man should quickly leave the abode taken up for attaining his objective, after achieving his objective. This will indicate his wisdom.

Durācārī Ca Duardṛṣṭirdurāvāsī Ca Darjana:.
Yanmaitrī Kriyatē Pumbhirnara: Śīghraṃ Vinaśyati..

2.19 Even intelligent and wise men are ruined after some time, if they remain in the company of immoral, sinful, wicked or cruel-natured persons. Such persons are like a coal mine where everything turns black. You must avoid friendship with such persons. In Chanakya's opinion, only the intelligent and wise person will suffer in such a relationship.

Samānē Śōbhatē Prīti: Rājñi Sēvā Ca Śōbhatē.
Vāṇijyaṃ Vyavahārēṣu Divyā Strī Śōbhatē Gṛhē..

2.20 Relations of affection and attraction are appropriate only with person of your status. The same also applies to official relations. For business having good public dealings and for home having a woman with superior qualities are appropriate. So, a man should have relations in a society with equals. Also only a government job offers stability, so it should be preferred over other jobs. In business, your success depends on public dealings and persuasiveness. Similarly, for a home, a talented and educated woman is adorable. Therefore, a man should always observe the above-cited things.

❑

Chapter 3

Kasya Dōṣa: Kulē Nāsti Vyādhinā Kō Na Pīḍita:.
Vyasańaṃ Kēna Na Prāptaṃ Kasya Saukhyaṃ Nirantaram..

3.1 There is no one in this world in whose family or lineage, there are no shortcomings or defects. A deep research will expose some shortcoming or the other. Similarly, there is no one in this world who is free from some illness or is totally happy and prosperous. So, everyone is gripped with sorrow, hardship, pain and illness. Nobody can escape from it. Happiness or sorrow and ups or downs come and go in everyone's life. So, a man should not feel helpless but face it with courage.

Ācāra: Kulamāakhyāti Dēṣamākhyāti Bhāṣaṇam.
Sambhrama: Snēhamākhyāti Vapurākhyāti Bhōjanam..

3.2 A man's behaviour, his thought process is the introduction to his family. From his speech, we can know about his motherland, from his behavior, we can learn about his attitude towards affection and respect and seeing his body, we can know about his food. In other words, his personality reflects his complete attitude. By observing a man's personality, an intelligent person can judge his good and bad qualities.

Sukulē Yōjayētkanyāṃ Putra Vidyāsu Yōjayēt.
Vyasanē Yōjayēcchatruṃ Mitraṃ Dharmē Niyōjayēt..

3.3 Expressing his opinion on an intelligent person, Chanakya says that he should marry his daughter in a respectable and suitable family. He should also provide the best possible education to his son and involve his friends in religious activities. It is necessary that the intelligent person ensures that his enemies are always trapped in difficulties. Then, they will never be able to create any hurdles or crisis for him. Undoubtedly Chanakya has shown signs of his political acumen in this shloka.

Durjanasya Ca Sarpasya Varaṃ Sarpō Na Durjana:.
Sarpō Daṃśati Kālēna Durjanastu Padē Padē..

3.4 Comparing a snake and a wicked person, Chanakya says that a snake bite is an unfortunate event. However, a wicked person will betray you at every step and unnecessarily hurts you. Therefore, if given a choice between the two, choose the snake without any hesitation.

Ētadarthaṃ Kulīnānāṃ Nṛpā: Kurvanti Saṅgraham.
Ādimadhyāvasānēṣu Na Tyajanti Ca Tē Nṛpam..

3.5 As intelligent and well-bred gentlemen do not abandon anyone in adverse and difficult circumstances, kings and scholars are always eager to shelter them. Such cultured and wise persons have the capability to face adverse circumstances with courage.

Pralayē Bhinnamaryādā Bhaavanti Kila Sāgarā:.
Sāgarā Bhēdamicchanti Pralayēpi Na Sādhava:..

3.6 Praising intelligent persons, Chanakya says that inspite of merger of several rivers into it, the sea remains calm but when there is a storm, then it breaks all boundaries and submerges large areas of the earth. But patient, mature and wise gentlemen maintain their cool even in adverse circumstances. That is, in any circumstance, they remain patient and try to find ways to resolve it with determination.

Mūrkhastu Parihartavya: Pratyakṣō Dvipada: Paśu:.
Bhianatti Vākśalyēna Adṛṣṭa: Kaṇṭakō Yathā..

3.7 A foolish person is like an animal with two legs. He can neither differentiate between right and wrong nor can he be taught anything. So, leave the company of such a person at the earliest. Like a thorn in the feet, even if not visible, hurts immensely, similarly, the foolish talk of a fool constantly pricks gentlemen.

Rūpayauvanasampanna: Viśālakulasambhavā:.
Vidyāhīnā Na Śōbhantē Nirgandhā Iva Kiṃśukā:..

3.8 Through this shloka, Chanakya has highlighted the importance of education. He says that as the fragrant and beautiful flower of the Dhak tree butea frondosa is never offered to gods/ goddesses, nor does it attract attention, similarly an illiterate but attractive person born in upper caste family cannot get respect. Looks, beauty, wealth, property, power, status and youth become graceful only when they are supported by education and wisdom.

Kōkilānāṃ Svarō Rūpaṃ Strīṇāṃ Rūpaṃ Pativratam.
Vidyā Rūpaṃ Kurūpāṇāṃ Kṣamā Rūpaṃ Tapasvinām..

3.9 On the importance of attributes, Chanakya says that like the black colour of the *koel* bird (cuckoo) becomes insignificant on account of its melodious voice; in other words, its melodious voice depicts its character. Similarly, loyalty towards her husband depicts a woman's image and beauty. An educated and intelligent ugly woman is much more beautiful than a gorgeous but a characterless woman. The attributes give her respect and status. The greatness of the hermit lies in his ability to forgive. Not losing their balance and patience, under any circumstances is the proof of their true devotion. These attributes enable assessment of the depth of their devotion.

Tyajēdēkaṃ Kulasyārthē Grāmasyārthē Kulaṃ Tyajēt.
Grāmaṃ Janapadasyārthē Ātmārthē Pṛthivīṃ Tyajēt..

3.10 According to Chanakya, if it is possible to protect the family by the relinquishment or sacrifice of one person, then it should be accepted. Similarly, if you can protect your village or society by the relinquishment or sacrifice of one family, then it is entirely appropriate. To save your state, a village or society can be sacrificed. But Chanakya also says that nothing is more important than you. So, if you need to sacrifice the whole world for your progress and protection, then do so without any hesitation. If you are yourself not there, then you have no use for your village, society or state.

Udyōgē Nāsti Dāridryaṃ Japatō Nāsti Pātakam.
Maunē Ca Kalahō Nāsti Nāsti Jāgaritē Bhayam..

3.11 Persons, who are vigorous or hard-working, do not face poverty; persons dedicated in praying are sinless; silence does not lead to arguments, rather creates a peaceful atmosphere. Similarly, a person, who is careful, alert and aware, will be fearless and no one can harm him.

Atirūpēṇa Vai Sītā Atigarvēṇa Rāvaṇa:.
Atidānaṃ Balirdatvā Ati Sarvatra Varjayēt..

3.12 Chanakya says that the excess of anything or act is harmful. According to him, Sita was kidnapped by Ravan because she was extraordinarily beautiful. Having excessive arrogance and ego caused the great scholar Ravan's death. On account of his excessive generosity, the demon king Bali lost everything and was sent to hell. It can, therefore, be said without any doubt that excesses lead to the end of man. So, avoid it.

Kō Hi Bhāra: Samarthānāṃ Kiṃ Dūraṃ Vyavasāyināṃ.
Kō Vidēśa: Savidyānāṃ Ka: Para: Priyavādinām..

3.13 No work is difficult or impossible for people who are powerful, capable and courageous. They complete whatever they resolve to do. For businessmen, no place is distant. They do not delay visiting any place. For scholars, no place is foreign. They are able to develop followers and friends on the strength of their education, intelligence and wisdom. Similarly, sweet talkers can convert even enemies to friends. So, they do not have any enemies.

Ēkēnāpi Suvṛkṣēṇa Puṣpitēna Sugandhinā.
Vāsitaṃ Tadvanaṃ Sarvaṃ Suputrēṇa Kulaṃ Tathā..

3.14 Praising virtuous persons, Chanakya says that like a single tree with fragrant flowers makes the whole forest aromatic, similarly, a single virtuous son born in the family reforms it.

Ēkēna Śuṣkavṛkṣēṇa Dahyamānēna Vihnanā.
Dahyatē Tadvanaṃ Sarvaṃ Kuputrēṇa Kulaṃ Tathā..

3.15 About a person devoid of any virtues, Chanakya says that as a single tree on fire can burn an entire forest, similarly, a virtueless son born in a status family can disgrace it by his acts. So, can a minor shortcoming in a scholar become a curse for him. Therefore, people should implant good ideas and traits in their children.

Ēkēnāpi Suputrēṇa Vidyāyuktēna Sādhunā.
Āhlāditaṃ Kulaṃ Sarvaṃ Yathā Candrēṇa Śarvarī..

3.16 As a single moon can dispel darkness—a job which cannot be done, even by hundreds of stars, similarly, a talented scholar, with character and soft speech, brings pride to the whole family. Nobody likes a dark night; similarly, a son devoid of any virtues is disliked by the family. Therefore, Chanakya says that it is appropriate to have a single virtuous son in the family rather than have several virtueless sons.

Kiṃ Jātairbahubhi: Putrai: Śōkasantāpakārakai:.
Varamēka: Kulālambī Yatra Viśrāmyatē Kulam..

3.17 In the context of a virtuous son, Chanakya says that a notorious and virtueless son pushes the family towards grief and dishonour, which leads to its ruin. On the contrary, a virtuous son, by his knowledge, wisdom and learning, earns place of pride, for the family in the society. Even though Ravan had hundreds of sons and grandsons, but being virtueless, they were all killed in the war. So, one virtuous son is better than several virtueless sons. He opens the door for the development and progress of the family.

Lālayēt Pañca Varṣāṇi Daśa Varṣāṇi Tāḍayēt.
Prāptē Tu Ṣōḍaśē Varṣē Putraṃ Mitravadācarēt..

3.18 On the responsibilities of a father towards his child, Chanakya says that for the first five years, he must be brought up with love and affection. For the next ten years, he must be brought up with strict discipline, because this is the period for the development of his personality. This period is like the foundation on which will rest the rest of his life. From the age of sixteen, he should be treated like a friend; guide him like a friend; settle his problems like a friend.

Upasargēnyacakrē Ca Durbhikṣē Ca Bhayāvahē.
Āsādhujanasamparkē Ya: Palāyēt Sa Jīvati..

3.19 The person, who escapes frightful disturbances, riots, attack by enemy, dreadful famines and company of wicked people is capable of defending his life. Through this shloka, Chanakya clarifies that for safe guarding his life, a person should change according to his circumstances.

Dharmārthakāmamōkṣāṇāṃ Yasyaikōpi Na Vidyatē.
Janma-Janmani Martyēṣu Maraṇaṃ Tasya Kēvalam..

3.20 Religion, wealth; sex and salvation have been termed as four important sects of life. Anyone, who does partake in any one of these sects, is wasting his life. Without any of these attributes, his life is like death, he has taken birth to die and to be reborn again. So, a man should not philander his precious life in sexual pleasures and luxury. Instead, he must adopt good qualities and earn goodwill.

Mūrkhā Yatra Na Pūjyantē Dhānyaṃ Yatra Susacintam.
Dampatyō: Kalahō Nāsti Tatra Śrī: Svayamāgatā..

3.21 According to Chanakya, in a state where the fools are not honoured, which is extraordinarily prosperous, in a house where there are no arguments between husband and wife, the presence of Goddess Lakshmi is certain. In such a place, there is no dearth of anything. All the members of the family live happily and harmoniously.

❑

Chapter 4

Āyu: Karma Ca Vittaṃ Ca Vidyā Nidhanamēva Ca.
Pañcaitāni Hi Sṛjyantē Garbhasthasyaiva Dēhina:..

4.1 Stressing on the need to act in life, Chanakya says that your age, activities, wealth, education and death is decided when you are still in your mothers womb. These five things are controlled by God; nobody can alter them. Yet man should keep making efforts.

Sādhubhyastē Nivartantē Putrā Mitrāṇi Bāndhavā:.
Yē Ca Tai: Saha Gantārastaddharmāt Sukṛtaṃ Kulam..

4.2 Chanakya says that when a person gets detached from society or becomes indifferent to attachment/wealth and becomes a saint, then his friends/relations, who see him off away from home and come back, usually get involved in attachment/wealth. But people, who adopt saintly practices and entire family follows virtuous conduct, reform their family.

Darśanadhyānasaṃsparśairmatsī Kūrmī Ca Pakṣiṇī.
Śiśuṃ Pālayatē Nityaṃ Tathā Sajjanasaṅgati:..

4.3 About gentlemanly and saintly persons, Chanakya says that like a fish raises her offsprings by sight, turtle by care and birds by touch, similarly, the company of gentlemen and qualified persons raises the level of common people. Their company opens the doors to God. Therefore, people should seek the company of saintly persons.

Yāvatsvasthō Hyayaṃ Dēhō Yāvanmṛtyuśca Dūrata:.
Tāvadātmahitaṃ Kuryāt Prāṇāntē Kiṃ Kariṣyati..

4.4 Describing religious activities and other good deeds, Chanakya says that religious activities, charity/pilgrimage, prayer/worship and fasting/attending discourses, etc. open the way to heaven. So for cleansing your soul, while you are hale and hearty, you must perform all these activities as per the proper practices, otherwise there will be nothing left after death.

Kāmadhēnuguṇā Vidyā Hyakālē Phaladāyinī.
Pravāsē Mātṛsadṛśī Vidyā Guptaṃ Dhanaṃ Smṛtam..

4.5 Sage Vashishtha had a cow named Kamdhenu, who could fulfil all his desires immediately. Chanakya has compared education to Kamdhenu. He says that like a person possessing Kamdhenu will never die of hunger, similarly, after attaining education, a man becomes capable to face any crisis. In a foreign place, education is like your mother, who will protect you at every step. Education is a hidden treasure, which no one can steal; on the contrary, the more you use it, the more it develops.

Varamēkō Guṇī Putrō Nirguṇaiśca Śatairapi:.
Ēkaścandrastamō Hanti Na Ca Tārā: Sahasraśa:..

4.6 Like a single moon can dispel darkness which even lacs of stars cannot do, a single bright and capable son is far better than hundred unmerited sons.

Mūrkhaścirāyurjātōapi Tasmājjātamṛtō Vara:.
Mṛta: Sa Cālpadu:Khāya Yāvajjīvaṃ Jaḍō Dahēt..

4.7 Chanakya says that a foolish and illiterate person only gives lifelong hardship and pain to his parents. It is, therefore, fit that such a son expires at birth rather than grow old. Even though it will grieve the parents for a short term but at least they will not have to suffer lifelong. History is also witness to several such foolish offsprings, who destroyed the mighty empires.

Kugrāmavāsa: Kulahīnasēvā Kubhōjanaṃ Krōdhamukhī Ca Bhāryā.
Putraśca Mūrkhō Vidhavā Ca Kanyā Vināgninā Ṣaṭ Pradaahanti Kāyam..

4.8 Residing in a bad or disreputed place, serving people of unknown background, eating bad food, a short-tempered wife, a foolish son and a widowed daughter—Chanakya says that these six reasons give heart rending pain like fire. So, gentlemen should take all possible measures to set them right.

Kiṃ Tayā Kriyatē Dhēnvā Yā Na Dōgdhrī Na Ca Gurviṇī.
akōrtha: Putrēṇa Jātēna Yō Na Vidvān Na Bhakitamān..

4.9 There is no point in keeping a barren cow, which does not give milk. Similarly, it is only right to relinquish an illiterate and disobedient son; otherwise, the family will have to bear untold hardships.

Saṃsāratāpadagdhānāṃ Trayō Viśrāntihētava:.
Apatyaṃ Ca Kalatraṃ Ca Satāṃ Saṅgatirēva Ca..

4.10 In this world, everyone is distressed by some sorrow. Such a person can feel happiness and peace only in the company of a virtuous son, loyal wife and gentlemen. So, Chanakya has advised people to keep company of scholars and gentlemen. According to him, humanities' happiness lies there.

Sakṛjjalpanti Rājāna: Sakṛjjalpanti Paṇḍitā:.
Sakṛt Kanyā: Pradīyantē Trīṇyētāni Sakṛtsakṛt..

4.11 According to Chanakya, a king's order is like a command and needs no repetition. Scholars and Pundits stick to what they say. A daughter's hand is given away in marriage once. So, any person, who wants do a good deed, must do it in one go.

Ēkākinā Tapō Dvābhyāṃ Paṭhanaṃ Gāyanaṃ Tribhi:.
Caturbhirgamanaṃ Kṣētraṃ Pañcabhirbabhubhī Raṇa:..

4.12 Chanakya has defined the number of people that must be involved in doing different types of tasks. Meditation, prayer-offerings and learning of lesson should be done alone. Involvement of more persons will create obstacles. Contrarily, studies are better done by two persons together. More than two persons will indulge in wasteful talk. For singing, three persons are adequate, whereas for travel, four persons are appropriate. For farming, five persons and for war, the largest number of persons are required.

Sā Bhāryā Yā Śucidrakṣā Sā Bhāryā Yā Pativratā.
Sā Bhāryā Yā Patiprītā Sā Bhāryā Satyavādinī..

4.13 In the context of an ideal wife, Chanakya says that a woman, who is pure, clever, wise; who is prudently devoted; who only loves her husband; who always speaks the truth and shuns lies, only that woman is respect/worthy and fit for the home/family.

Aputrasya Gṛhaṃ Śūnyaṃ Diśa: Śūnyāstvabāndhavā:.
Mūrkhasya Hṛdayaṃ Śūnyaṃ Sarvaśūnyā Daridratā:..

4.14 As a home is desolate without children, similarly, a man feels lonely without friends and relations. But stupid, poor and poverty-stricken men always have selfish motives, so they do not have any feelings of love, affection or sympathy. Therefore, they live in isolation as everyone stays away from them.

Anabhyāsē Viṣaṃ Śāstramajīrṇē Bhōjanaṃ Viṣam.
Daridrasya Viṣaṃ Gōṣṭhī Vaddhasya Taruṇī Viṣam..

4.15 According to Chanakya, without practice, even scholars cannot recite manuscripts properly and will be mocked. For them, this insult will be more painful than death. So, for a scholar, who does not practise regularly, the manuscript is like poison. Similarly, a person, whose digestion is weak or who cannot digest food properly, even delicacies are like poison for him. Because in meetings and seminars, the poor person is always insulted, so for him such places are like poison. For an aged person, a young wife is like poison. In such circumstances, the young wife's behaviour is very painful and insulting for the aged man.

Tyajēt Dharmaṃ Dayāhīnaṃ Vidyāhīnaṃ Guruṃ Tyajēt.
Tyajēt Krōdhamukhīṃ Bhāryāṃ Ni:Snēhān Bāndhavāṃstyajēt..

4.16 Through this shloka, Chanakya cautions mankind to never accept a religion, which is bereft of compassion; not to consider a person as a Guru who is not a scholar; not take an extremely short-tempered woman as a wife. Similarly, never consider children, who lack affection; friends, who do not value friendship, dear and trustworthy.

Adhvā Jarā Manuṣyāṇāṃ Vājināṃ Bandhanaṃ Jarā.
Amaithunaṃ Jarā Strīṇāṃ Vastrāṇāmātapō Jarā..

4.17 Regarding aging, Chanakya says that walking lost in thought for long periods, keeping horses tied to their holders, denying women sexual pleasures and drying clothes in sun for very long signal the arrival of old age. So, avoid them.

Ka: Kāla: Kāni Mitrāṇi Kō Dēśa: Kau Vyayagamau.
Kāścāhaṃ Kā Ca Mē Śakitariti Cintyaṃ Muhurmuhu:..

4.18 According to Chanakya, people should take precautions regarding certain important matters. How are we doing, who are our friends and foes, how is our residence, how much is our income and expenditure, what is our strength—they must focus on all these matters. People, who take care of all these matters, are never unsuccessful.

Janitā Cōpanētā Ca Yastu Vidyāṃ Prayacchati.
Annadātā Bhayatrātā Pañcaitē Pitara: Smṛtā:..

4.19 Chanakya has considered the Mother who gives birth to you, the Brahmin, who performs your religious thread ceremony, the Guru, who teaches you, the person, who feeds you and one who dispels fear, having the status of your Father. He says man should be indebted to them and should always respect/honour them. He is reborn again on account of them.

Rājapatnī Gurō: Patnī Mitrapatnī Tathaiva Ca.
Patnīmātā Svamātā Ca Pa`icaitā Mātara: Smṛtā:..

4.20 Chanakya says that man has five mothers— the King's wife, Guru's wife, friend's wife, wife's mother and your own mother. He says man should extend due respect/honour to them. Anyone, who shows evil intent against them or disrespects them, goes to hell.

Agnirdēvō Dvijāatīnāṃ Munīnāṃ Hṛdi Daïvatam.
Pratimā Svalpabuddhīnāṃ Sarvatra Samadarśina:..

4.21 Brahmin, Kshatriya and Vaishya are born twice—once from the mother's womb and, the second time, when they attain knowledge from the Guru. They are, therefore, called dual castes. Their idol is Sun God. In contrast, the Gods of saints reside in their hearts. The Gods of people with limited intelligence exist in statues. But for very broad-minded people, the Gods exist in every particle in the world.

❑

Chapter 5

Gururagnirdvijātīnāṃ Varṇānāṃ Brāhmaṇō Guru:.
Patirēva Guru: Strīṇāṃ Sarvasyābhyāgatō Guru:..

5.1 Regarding Guru, Chanakya says that for Brahmin, Kshatriya and Vaishya, fire is like their Guru. Since the Brahmin is superior amongst all the castes, so he is the Guru for all. Similarly, for a woman, her husband is her worship deity and Guru. But Chanakya has called the guest as most respectful and worshipable. In this context, he says that a guest only desires hospitality. He has no other vested interest, so he is most superior.

Yathā Caturbhi: Kanakaṃ Parīkṣyatē Nigharṣaṇacchēdanatāpatāḍanai:.
Yathā Caturbhi: Puruṣa: Parīkṣyatē Tyāgēna Śīlēna Guṇēna Karmaṇā..

5.2 Chanakya says that to test the purity of gold, it is heated at high temperature; it is tapped, hammered and cut. That gives it the glitter. Similarly, an honest person is tested for purity by his acts of donation, good deeds, virtuosity, sacrifice and behaviour. Any person, who possesses all these qualities, glitters like gold.

Tāvad Bhayēṣu Bhētavyaṃ Yāvad Bhayamanāgatam.
Āgataṃ Tu Bhayaṃ Dṛṣṭvā Prahartavyamaśaṅkayā..

5.3 How should an intelligent person act in a crisis—in this context, expressing his opinion, Chanakya says that as long as he is free of difficulties, worries and crises, he should fear them. But once he is surrounded by them, then he should face them fearlessly, courageously and patiently. Only then can he defeat and escape from them.

Ēkōdarasamudbhūtā Ēkanakṣatrajātakā:.
Na Bhavanti Samā: Śīlē Yathā Badarakāṇṭakā:..

5.4 Citing an example of diversity of human nature, Chanakya says that berries and thorns growing on the same tree and branch have different characteristics. The consumption of berries gives a man sweetness and satisfaction, whereas the pricking of thorns gives him pain and irritation. Similarly, children born under the influence of the same planet or born at the same time from the same womb, have different characteristics. So a man should understand this fully, only then can he attain peace.

Ni:Spṛhō Nādhikārī Syānnākāmī Maṇḍanapriya:.
Nāvidagdha: Priyaṃ Brūyāt Sphuṭavaktā Na Vañcaka:..

5.5 On the character of a person, Chanakya says that a person, who demands his rights, is greedy. A person, who places importance on beauty and make-up, is lustful. Foolish people by nature are not soft-spoken. Contrarily, persons who are frank and truthful do not have even an iota of cunning, deceit and craftiness.

Mūrkhāṇāṃ Paṇḍitā Dvēṣyā Adhanānāṃ Mahādhanā:.
Vārāṅganā: Kulastrīṇāṃ Subhagānāṃ Ca Durbhagā:..

5.6 Discussing human nature, Chanakya says that no one is pleased to see anyone superior to him; rather he envies and hates him. Foolish people hate scholars due to envy; so they ill-treat them. On account of envy only, lazy and poor people develop enmity towards the affluent. Similarly, prostitutes envy loyal women and widows envy married women. Even though such envious behaviour should be overlooked by scholars from fools, affluent from poor, loyal women from prostitutes and married women from widows, they also mutually find faults to prove their superiority under the influence of foolishness and envy.

Ālasyōpahatā Vidyā Parahastagatā: Striya:.
Alpabījaṃ Hataṃ Kṣētraṃ Sainyamanāyakam..

5.7 According to Chanakya, laziness and irregular practice corrupts the intelligence of scholars and ruins their knowledge. Women under the influence of others are soon ruined. Lack or shortage of seeds results in lower crop output. Similarly, in the absence of the commander, the army can never win a war. Thus, in order to get superior results, the importance of regular practice must be understood.

Abhyāsāddhāryatē Vidyā Kulaṃ Śīlēna Dhāryatē.
Guṇēna Jñāyatē Tvārya: Kōpō Nētrēṇa Gamyatē..

5.8 Chanakya says that only by constant practice, knowledge can be retained. Similarly, only by his acts, behaviour and nature, a man can attain honour, respect and glory for his family. For this, being born in an upper caste, having higher status and being rich is not material. Good people are recognised by their traits, whereas eyes show anger.

Vittēna Rakṣyatē Dharmō Vidyā Yōgēna Rakṣyatē.
Mṛdunā Rakṣyatē Bhūpa: Sannāryā Rakṣyatē Gṛham..

5.9 On the importance of wealth, meditation, soft speech and loyal woman, Chanakya says that wealth safeguards religion, meditation safeguards education, soft and gentle speech safeguards the king and loyal woman safeguards the household.

Anyathā Vēdapāṇḍityaṃ Śāstramācāramanyathā.
Anyathā Kuvaca: Śāntaṃ Lōkā: Kliśyanti Cānyathā..

5.10 The person, who criticises knowledge of scriptures, the superiority of manuscripts and truthful persons, faces extreme hardships in this and other world. Such persons are neither able to gain respect/honour in society or reap benefits of their prayers after their death. The persons who keep their company, also meet the same fate, in the same measure.

Dāridryanāśanaṃ Dānaṃ Śīlaṃ Durgatināśanam.
Ajñānanāśinī Prajñā Bhāvanā Bhayaanāśinī..

5.11 In this shloka about donation, modesty, knowledge and courtesy, Chanakya says that donation is an effective means of alleviating poverty. Modesty eliminates degradation and hardships. Knowledge ends a man's stupidity and ignorance, whereas courtesy destroys a man's fear. So, for living peacefully, a man should develop and imbibe all the four qualities.

Nāsti Kāmasamō Vyādhirnāsti Mōhasamō Ripu:.
Nāsti Kōpasamō Vahnirnāsti Jñānātparaṃ Sukham..

5.12 Describing disorders like lust, infatuation and anger in a man's life, Chanakya says that lust is a man's most powerful enemy. It is such an untreatable disease under the influence of which a man loses his wisdom, as well as his health deteriorates rapidly. Infatuation destroys a man like an enemy. It was infatuation for a son which caused the destructive war of Mahabharata. Similarly, anger is like a wild fire, whose flames repeatedly singe man. It affects man's mind/brain every moment. Chanakya says that knowledge is the best weapon for destroying these disorders. According to him, only knowledge can subdue these disorders and lead to peaceful existence.

Janmamṛtyu Hi Yātyēkō Bhunaktyēka: Śubhāśubham.
Narakēṣu Patatyēka Ēkō Yāti Parāṃ Gatim..

5.13 Inspite of having so many relations, friends, wife, son, etc. in this world, a man is basically alone. He is born alone and has to depart alone from this world. He alone has to bear the consequences of all his good and bad deeds. He has no partner in this. Happiness and sorrow are only his; they will affect him only. He has to travel the life's journey towards heaven alone.

Tṛṇaṃ Brahmavida: Svargastṛṇaṃ Śūrasya Jīvitam.
Jitākṣasya Tṛṇaṃ Nārī Ni:Spṛhasya Tṛṇaṃ Jagat..

5.14 For a Brahmin, who gives importance to acts, even the pleasures of heaven are useless; whereas, for a Kshatriya, who takes pride and feels honoured in taking risks, he is least bothered about his life. Any man, who exercises control over all his senses, remains unmoved by the looks/beauty of a young woman. He is never affected by disorders like lust, anger, greed, liquor, infatuation, etc. Similarly, for a person, who is detached from worldly matters and is without greed, even precious stones are like straws.

Vidyā Mitraṃ Pravāsēṣu Bhāryā Mitraṃ Gṛhēṣu Ca.
Vyădhitasyauṣadhaṃ Mitraṃ Dharmō Mitraṃ Mṛtasya Ca..

5.15 Defining a true friend, Chanakya says that for a person going abroad, education is his true friend and for the family, a loyal wife is a true friend. For a sick person, his medicine is a true friend. Since after death only a person's acts and religious beliefs count, so religion is his true well-wisher. Therefore, a man should perform good deeds while living, so that he does not face hardships after death.

Vṛthā Vṛṣṭi: Samudrēṣu Vṛthā Tṛptēṣu Bhōjanam.
Vṛthāṃ Dānaṃ Dhanāḍhyēṣu Vṛthā Dīpō Divāpi Ca..

5.16 Explaining the purpose and benefits of donation, Chanakya says that like rain serves no purpose over a sea, a candle is useless in daylight, it is useless to feed a person who is not hungry and give alms to a rich person. Chanakya says that rain is required in fields and candle is required in darkness; food must be fed to a hungry person and alms must be given to the poor. One can only derive benefits from such donations and good deeds.

Nāsti Mēghasamaṃ Tōyaṃ Nāsti Cātmasarma Balam.
Nāsti Cakṣu:Samaṃ Tējō Nāsti Dhānyasamaṃ Priyam..

5.17 Chanakya has considered rain water to be most pure and pious from the viewpoint of health and usefulness. Since your inner strength can control senses and body, so he has considered the inner strength to be the most superior. Animates see the world created by God through their eyes, so there is no greater vision than eye-sight. There is nothing more tasty and relishing than grain. It satiates the mankind's hunger and gives him strength. Mankind never tires of consuming it.

Adhanā Dhanamicchanti Vācaṃ Caiva Catuṣpadā:.
Mānavāṃ Svargamicchanti Mōkṣamicchanti Dēvatā:..

5.18 On diverse desires of different persons, Chanakya says that poor and poverty-stricken persons desire wealth; animals desire speech; ordinary persons are obsessed with the idea of going to heaven; God men and hermits only seek relinquishment. Similarly, mankind is distressed with having some desire or the other and continuously thinks about it, so much so that they even consider what they possess to be inferior.

Satyēna Dhāryatē Pṛthivī Satyēna Tapatē Ravi:.
Satyēna Vāti Vāyuśca Sarvaṃ Satyē Pratiṣṭhitam..

5.19 Explaining the power of truth, through this shloka, Chanakya says that the foundation of a Brahmin's spirit/soul is truth. This world is surviving on truth alone. The glow of truth is illuminated in the form of the Sun in the sky. The power of truth moves the air, brings about the changes of day-night and the weather. Explaining the value of truth in detail, Chanakya says that the power of truth has given stability to this universe. The destruction of truth leads to upheavals and the universe submerges under water. Chanakya says that, therefore, mankind should believe in truth and behave accordingly.

Calā Lakṣmīścalā: Prāṇāścalaṃ Jīvita-Yauvanam.
Calācalē Ca Saṃsārē Dharma Ēkō Hi Niścala:..

5.20 On religion, Chanakya says that even though this world is destructible, religion can never be destroyed. Wealth, youth life can be destroyed one by one. However, religion is indestructible, immortal and eternal; nobody can destroy it. Even though in his lifetime, man amasses invaluable things/wealth and is surrounded by relations, after death, he loses everything except religion. So, he must follow the path of religion. The allurements of the worldly destructible things distract him and try to divert him from the path of religion, so he must sacrifice them. As the darkness is dispelled by Sun's rays, similarly, practice of religion dispels all the sorrows of man, in this as well as in the other world.

Nārāṇāṃ Nāpitō Dhūrta: Pakṣiṇāṃ Caiva Vāyasa:.
Catuṣpadāṃ Śṛgālastu Strīṇāṃ Dhūrtā Ca Mālinī..

5.21 In this shloka, Chanakya has identified the cunning. He says that amongst men, the barber is the most cunning. Likewise, in birds, the crow, in animals, the jackal and in women, the female gardener is most cunning and crafty. They are always attempting to harm others. So, gentlemen must avoid the company and friendship of such persons.

❑

Chapter 6

Śrutvā Dharmaṃ Vijānāti Śrutvā Tyajati Durmatim.
Śrutvā Jñānāmavāpnōti Śrutvā Mōkṣamavāpnuyāt..

6.1 In this shloka, Chanakya has clarified the importance of study and listening of the Vedic manuscripts. He says that to understand the depth of religion, the knowledge of the Vedic manuscripts is essential. Through them, man can imbibe the essence of religion in life. Vedic knowledge can even move the man's sin-filled mind towards righteousness. By its influence, even an ordinary man can attain superiority. The power of Vedic knowledge enables the saints to undertake the welfare of the world and reach heaven after death.

Like the study of the Vedic manuscripts is extremely beneficial, likewise listening to its recitation purifies the mind. So, if the study of the manuscripts is not possible for men, then they should listen to its recitation. This will enable them to understand the Vedic knowledge in greater depth.

Pakṣiṇāṃ Kākaścāṇḍāla: Paśūnāṃ Caiva Kukkura:.
Munīnāṃ Kōpī Cāṇḍāla: Sarvēṣāṃ Caiva Nindaka:..

6.2 On critics, Chanakya says that even though in birds the crow, in animals the dog and a sinner saint are the most evil and irreligious, the critic is even a greater sinner and of a wretched nature. Even though the critic gains nothing by criticising, he enjoys it. His sins keep adding up by criticising and a day comes when his sins destroy him. So, Chanakya has cautioned men against criticising.

Bhasmanā Śudhyatē Kāṃsyaṃ Tāmramamlēna Śudhyati.
Rajasā Śudhyatē Nārī Nadī Vēgēna Śudhyati..

6.3 On the pathetic condition of women, Chanakya has written an appropriate shloka. He says that as by rubbing ash a brass utensil shines, as dried mango powder purifies a copper utensil, as a swiftly flowing river remains clean, similarly, after menstruation, a woman becomes pure and pious and is able to conceive. But women who don't have menstruation or are unable or incapable to conceive, they do not get due respect in the society.

Bhraman Sampūjyatē Rājā Bhraman Sampūjyatē Dvija:.
Bhraman Sampūjyatē Yōgī Strī Bhramantī Vinaśyati..

6.4 In this shloka, Chanakya says that a king, a Brahmin and an ascetic who tour are respected. On the contrary, a woman who wanders around is considered corrupt and immoral in the society. Explaining in detail, Chanakya says that it is the duty of a king to know the difficulties being faced by his people. How his officers behave with the people and what actions they are taking for their welfare? So to get first-hand information, he should travel incognito. If the Brahmin keeps travelling, he is never short of followers. Also his status in the society rises day by day. Travelling by saints and ascetic enables them to spread their knowledge and wisdom amongst the masses. Thus, the backward and ignorant people who listen to them develop righteousness. But for a woman, who travels without any purpose draws herself closer to hell.

Needy and resourceless women can fall into bad company and loose their character and respect. So, they should refrain from the travelling needlessly.

Tādṛśī Jāyatē Buddhirvyavasāyōpi Tādṛśa:.
Sahāyāstādṛśā Ēva Yādṛśī Bhavitavyatā..

6.5 "What is destined cannot be changed by anybody": this saying has often been heard in different sections of the society from time immemorial. This saying illustrates the superiority of fate and its impact. Chanakya has probably written this shloka after a deep study of this saying. On his thoughts about fate, he says that ones wisdom is dictated by one's fate at birth. His life, actions, situations—everything is decided by fate. He also gets relations and friends as destined by his fate. Man gets only what he is destined to get. But Chanakya also believes that man should not be entirely dependent on fate. Man's duty is to make efforts, so he should always strive to do so.

Kāla: Pacati Bhūtāni Kāla: Saṃharatē Prajā:.
Kāla: Suptēṣu Jāgarti Kālō Hi Duratikrama:..

6.6 On time, Chanakya says that time or death is most powerful. It is so powerful that it can destruct anything in this universe in no time. Even when universal destruction causes it to disappear under water, the time is ticking. Time cycle is perpetually in motion. Against it even the most knowledgeable persons, scholars and good souls become helpless, the brave and bold Kshatriya are defeated. All the four life stages of mankind conform to time. It is impossible for everyone to win over time. It is, therefore, imperative that mankind remains righteous and habitually performs good deeds. Through good deeds only he can set right his life in the next world.

Na Paśyati Ca Janmāndha: Kāmāndhō Naiva Paśyati.
Na Paśyati Madōnmattō Hyarthī Dōṣān Na Paśyati..

6.7 A person born blind cannot see anything. But a person, who is blinded by lust, also loses his ability to think inspite of having vision that person acts in demeaning and censurable manner in large gatherings. Similarly, a person addicted to liquor is also categorised as blind. Intoxicated by liquor, people lose their mental balance and their thinking ability. On account of his useless and meaningless talk, he is criticized and scoffed. Likewise, Chanakya has called a selfish and sinning person blind. According to him, such a person never thinks twice in causing hurt/loss to anyone, to fulfil his selfish interests. For him, there is no difference in sin and good deed. For him in front of his vested interest, everything else is inferior.

Svayaṃ Karma Karōtyātmā Svayaṃ Tatphalamaśnutē.
Svayaṃ Bhramati Saṃsārē Svayaṃ Tasmād Vimucyatē..

6.8 As Lord Shri Krishna preached Arjuna in *Gita* on ones deeds, likewise through this shloka, Chanakya in the *avatar* of Krishna preaches the mankind in the *avatar* of Arjuna. He says that everyone reaps according to his deeds, good or bad. His deeds only bind him to wealth. He is born repeatedly in this world in different forms according to his deeds. Even though a man is free to act, he cannot reap as he desires. Man can only control his actions; but only the Lord has the power to reward him for his deeds. So, for his salvation, a man must keep trying himself.

Rājā Rāṣṭrakṛtaṃ Pāpaṃ Rājña: Pāpaṃ Purōhita:.
Bhartā Ca Strīkṛtaṃ Pāpaṃ Śiṣyapāpaṃ Gurustathā..

6.9 In the context of sins, Chanakya says that only the king has to bear for the sins committed by his subjects. The sins committed by the king are borne by the family priest. The sins of the wife affect the husband and that of the student affect the Guru. So Chanakya has stressed on the necessity to contain the sins in the kingdom. According to him, it is the duty of the king to eliminate all kinds of sins in his kingdom; he should not allow the spread of arbitrariness and evil. This will ensure that the people in his kingdom lead a fearless life and the king shall reap its rewards. Thus, he has stressed on the necessity to restrict sins and to establish a religious reign.

Ṛṇakartā Pitā Śatru: Mātā Ca Vyabhicāriṇī.
Bhāryā Rūpavatī Śatru: Putra: Śatrupaṇḍita:..

6.10 Chanakya has composed this shloka to explain as to who is the true enemy of man. According to him, a father, who leaves debt on his children, is their true enemy. An adulteress is the enemy of her children. Similarly, an extraordinarily beautiful woman is the enemy of her husband; a foolish and obstinate son ruins the father. Contrarily, an industrious father, a religious mother, a loyal wife and an intelligent son are all the true well-wishers of a man. In fact, their support leads the man towards the righteous path.

Lubdhamarthēna Gṛhṇīyāt Stabdhmajaṃlikarmaṇā.
Mūrkhaṃ Chandōnuvṛttēna Yathārthatvēna Paṇḍitam..

6.11 In this shloka, Chanakya has told of ways to control diverse persons. He says that a person, who is greedy by nature, can be controlled by allurement only. An obstinate and arrogant person can be controlled by politeness. If a foolish and brainless person's wishes are fulfilled, then he can be easily controlled. To mould an intelligent person, he must be made aware of the facts. Thus, after analysing the weakness and the needs of a man, Chanakya has given the Guru Mantras to control them.

Varaṃ Na Rājyaṃ Na Kurājarājyaṃ
Varaṃ Na Mitraṃ Na Kumitramitram.
Varaṃ Na Śiṣyō Na Kuśiṣyaśiṣyō
Varaṃ Na Dārā Na Kudāradārā:..

6.12 A state in which sins and sinners abound, instead of staying there, it is better to stay in an isolated place. It is much better to be without a friend rather than have a friend, who is untrustworthy, cunning and evil; because such a friend will ruin you anytime. Similarly, it is much better to be without a characterless pupil or an adulteress wife. Such people are like coal that stain even gentlemen, who provide them support. A person, who stays away from them, is able to enjoy the pleasures of life.

Kurājarājyēna Kuta: Prajāsukhaṃ
Kumitramitrēṇa Kutōsti Nirvṛtti:.
Kudāradāraiśca Kutō Gṛhē Rati:
Kuśiṣyamadhyāpayata: Kutō Yaśa:..

6.13 In this shloka, Chanakya has expressed his invaluable views on the king, friend, pupil and wife. He says that in a kingdom, where the king is evil, unreligious and sinner, the people can never live in peace. Therefore, people should only reside in a kingdom whose king is righteous. It is useless to expect support or affection from a friend, who is deceitful and treacherous. Befriend only a person who is able and trustworthy. You can never expect love and pleasure from a woman, who is disloyal and cunning. Therefore, you must marry a woman who is well-mannered and from a well-bred family. It will enhance the pleasures of married life. Similarly, characterless and irreligious pupils will always bring defame. It is much better not to have them.

Siṃhādēkaṃ Bakādēkaṃ Śikṣēccatvāri Kukkuṭāt.
Vāyasātpañca Śikṣēcca Paṭ Śunastrīṇi Gardabhāt..

6.14 In the scriptures, it is stated that man should gracefully accept learning, from wherever he gets it. Chanakya agrees with it. Through this shloka addressing man, Chanakya says that God has definitely given some quality or the other to every living thing. So, any qualities of even foolish persons or animals should be accepted without any hesitation or shame. He says that man should accept one quality each from lion and stork, three from donkey, four from cock, five from crow and six from dog.

Prabhūtaṃ Kāryamalpaṃ Vā Yannara: Kartumicchati.
Sarvārambhēṇa Tatkāryaṃ Siṃhādēkaṃ Pracakṣatē..

6.15 According to Chanakya, the lion is gifted with an important quality, which man should imbibe. He says that if a man takes responsibility for any work, then he should fulfil it with sincerity and courage. However, before taking up the responsibility, a man should introspect on his strengths and weaknesses. Thereafter, he should make efforts to complete it with full sincerity and wisdom. This will bring him fame and respect. Contrarily, men who dither to complete the assumed work or misguide others, nobody trusts them again.

Indriyāṇi Ca Saṃyamya Bakavat Paṇḍitō Nara:.
Dēśakālabalaṃ Jñātvā Sarvakāryāṇi Sādhayēt..

6.16 The stork has the quality of concentration and patience. In this shloka, Chanakya has suggested imbibing this quality. He says that like the stork focuses patiently its sights on its prey and expels all other thoughts from its mind, an intelligent and wise person should control all his senses, focus and complete his work. This will ensure hundred per cent success.

Pratyutthānaṃ Ca Yuddhaṃ Ca Saṃvibhāgaṃ Ca Bandhuṣu.
Svayamākramya Bhuktaṃ Ca Śikṣēccatvāri Kukkuṭāt..

6.17 Chanakya has stressed intelligent and wise persons on imbibing four qualities from the cock. Getting up at a fixed time; being ever ready for a fight; sharing fairly with friends/relations and sexually satisfying its hen. Like the cock rises early daily and attends to its chores, similarly, a man should also rise early and attend to his chores. While on one hand, it will keep him healthy, on the other, he will be able to complete his tasks on time. It is in the nature of the cock to be ever ready for a fight. So, a man should also be ready to fight his enemies with full courage. The cock believes in sharing. Accordingly, a man should also give away everyone's share at the right time. The denial or lack of sexual pleasures drives a woman towards disloyalty. Therefore, like the cock, a man should keep his wife sexually satisfied, so that she remains loyal.

Gūḍhaṃ Ca Maithunaṃ Dhāṣaṭyaṃ Kālē Kālē Ca Saṅgraham.
Apramattamaviśvāsaṃ Pañca Śikṣēcca Vāyasāt..

6.18 Chanakya has stated that the crow is gifted with five qualities—performing sex in private; being wicked and adamant; having nature to store; never being lazy and never trusting anyone—which a man should imbibe. Like the crow has sex in private, man should also have sex in private. This ensures he retains his esteem and respect. To repel his enemies man should learn the wickedness and obstinacy of the crow. He can then destroy his enemies. The nature to store can pull man through difficult times with determination and courage. The crow is never lazy, so, a man should shun his laziness and concentrate on his tasks. This will ensure his success. Never trusting anyone is the strongest quality of the crow. If a man adopts this, then he protects himself fully, and nobody can harm him.

Bahvāśī Svalpasantuṣṭa: Sunidrō Laghucētana:.
Svāmibhaktaśca Śūraśca Ṣaḍētē Śvānatō Guṇā:..

6.19 Having a large appetite, being satisfied with less in adversity, having a sound sleep, remaining alert even while sleeping, facing the enemy with loyalty and courage—the dog has these six qualities. Chanakya says that these six qualities are superlative for a man. He says that if a man imbibes these qualities, then he remains fit as well as he experiences mental peace and contentment.

Suśrāantōpi Vahēd Bhāraṃ Śītōṣṇaṃ Na Ca Paśyati.
Santuṣṭaścaratē Nityaṃ Trīṇi Śikṣēcca Gardabhāt..

6.20 According to Chanakya, even the symbol of foolishness, the donkey, has three qualities. Toiling tirelessly, not being bothered by hot or cold weather, being patient and contented—the presence of these qualities makes a man's life worthwhile. A man should tirelessly work like a donkey. This will ensure his success. Not being bothered about hot or cold weather will condition his body and he will always remain fit. Similarly, by being patient and contented, he can care for his family even with less and be happy.

Ya Ētān Viṃśatiguṇānācariṣyati Mānava:.
Kāryāvasthāsu Sarvāsu Ajēya: Sa Bhaviṣyati..

6.21 In conclusion, Chanakya says that anyone who adopts all the twenty qualities, his life will be filled with happiness and success. He will be able to enslave happiness and continue to rise in life.

❑

Chapter 7

Arthanāśaṃ Manastāpaṃ Gṛhē Duścaritāni Ca.
Vañcanaṃ Cāapamānaṃ Ca Matimānna Prakāśayēt..

7.1 Chanakya believes that endurance is an essential quality in an intelligent person. According to him, a person should not reveal to anyone sorrow of loss of his wealth, having an evil wife or being insulted by anyone else. For this, he must be enduring. Endurance will save him from humiliation in front of others. Therefore, he must imbibe the endurance quality and bear all the above adversities quietly.

Dhana-Dhānyaprayōgēṣu Vidyāsaṅgrahaṇēṣu Ca.
Āhārē Vyavahārē Ca Tyaktalajja: Sukhī Bhavēt..

7.2 In this shloka, Chanakya clarifies that those people, who hesitate in the activities of buying-selling, teaching, eateries and money lending, will face lot of problems and difficulties. It is, therefore, appropriate that people involved in the above-cited activities should never hesitate.

Santōṣāmṛta-Tṛptānāṃ Yatsukhaṃ Śāntacētasām.
Na Ca Tad Dhanalubdhānāmitaścētaśca Dhāvatām..

7.3 There is no end to a man's desires and lusts. The fulfilment of one's desire leads to creation of several other desires.

Gradually, these desires overpower him and draw him towards a sinful life. A man should imbibe the two qualities of patience and contentment. These will ensure that he is at peace with himself and is satisfied. This is the simplest and easiest path to attaining happiness in life. In contrast, people, who are greedy and have vested interests, never experience true happiness during their lifetime. They are always under mental stress and remain disturbed. So, a man should stay away from such traits.

Santōṣastriṣu Kartavya: Svadārē Bhōjanē Dhanē.
Triṣu Caiva Na Kartavyōdhyayanē Tapadānayō:..

7.4 A woman, food and wealth provide tremendous satisfaction to man. Chanakya also accepts this fact. He says that one's wife, even if she is ugly or beautiful, evil or amiable, foolish or intelligent—should not be deserted. If he is satisfied with her, then he will be free from mental tension forever. A man should never reject food just because it is not tasty. He should gladly accept whatever food he gets, be it simple or fit for royals. Similarly, he should feel satisfied with whatever he earns through labour. In addition, Chanakya also advises man to stay ahead in donating, praying and learning.

Viprayōrvipravahnayōśca Dampatyō: Svāmibhṛtyayō:.
Antarēṇa Na Gantavyaṃ Halasya Vṛṣabhasya Ca..

7.5 Chanakya says that it is important that you should not pass between two people in discussion. He says that there is the fear of a calamity if you pass through two Brahmins, Brahmin and his prayer fire, a couple, employer and his employee and bull and plough. You should side step, instead of passing through.

**Pādābhyāṃ Na Spṛśēdagniṃ Guru Brāhmaṇamēva Ca.
Naiva Gāṃ Na Kumārīṃ Ca Na Vṛddhaṃ Na Śiśuṃ Tathā..**

7.6 Chanakya says that fire, guru, Brahmin, cow, girl, aged and child must be respected and honoured. Therefore, they must never be touched with your feet. Anyone doing so is a fool and comes to grief.

**Śakaṭaṃ Pañcahastēna Daśahastēna Vājinam.
Hastī Śatahastēna Dēśatyāgēna Durjanam..**

7.7 Friendship with an evil person is very damaging and full of pitfulls falls. So man should stay away from his company. Chanakya expressing his view, says that it is in your interest if you stay five steps away from a bullock cart, ten steps away from a horse and hundred steps away from an elephant. But Chanakya has considered an evil person even more dangerous than all of them. So, he has suggested that a gentleman should not hesitate to even leave the country to stay away from an evil person, otherwise, he cannot escape from his downfall for long.

**Hastī Aṅkuśahastēna Vājī Hastēna Tāḍyatē.
Śṛṅgī Laguhastēna Khaṅgastēna Durjana:..**

7.8 On the tendency and ways to control an evil person, Chanakya says that like an elephant is controlled by an iron hook, horse by a whip and horned animals by a stick, to control an evil person, one needs to use a sword. Explaining in detail, Chanakya says that an evil person has a very low mentality. He is always eagerly scheming to harm others. It is impossible to change such people by love, affection and knowledge. There are instances when the evil person even crosses all limits. In such circumstances, a gentleman should use the sword for his self-defence.

Tuṣyanti Bhōjanē Viprā Mayūrā Ghanagarjitē.
Sādhava: Parasampattau Khala: Paravipattiṣu..

7.9 A Brahmin loves his food, so ample delicious food gives him fulfilment. A peacock is pleased to see the clouds; its thundering prompts it to dance. This dancing satisfies it. A gentleman is never jealous of others grandeur, opulence, progress and happiness, rather he is satisfied with their meager means. On the other hand, an evil and cruel person is satisfied in harming others. They feel elated seeing others in crisis.

Anulōmēna Balinaṃ Pratilōmēna Durjanam.
Ātmatulyabalaṃ Śatruṃ Vinayēna Balēna Vā..

7.10 In this shloka, Chanakya reveals an important strategic saying. It also has a hidden meaning. He says that a strong person cannot be won over by force. You should control him by conduct favourable to him. An evil enemy should be defeated by adopting conduct unfavourable to him. Whereas an equal enemy can be won over by a combination of humility and force.

Bāhuvīryaṃ Balaṃ Rājñō Brāhmaṇō Brahmavid Balī.
Rūpayauvanamādhuryaṃ Strīṇāṃ Balamuttamam..

7.11 What is the true strength of man? By which inner strength can a man make others bow before him? In this context, Chanakya's statement has lot of depth. He says that a king's strength lies in his arms, with which he destroys his enemy. A Brahmin's strength is inherent in his knowledge of the scriptures, through which he can defeat even the greatest scholar. A woman's strength lies in her beauty, youth and sweet talk. Even while being delicate, through them she has the power to make any one bow before her. So, a man should understand his strengths completely.

Nātyantaṃ Saralairbhāvyaṃ Gatvā Paśya Vanasthalīm.
Chidyantē Saralāstatra Kubjāstiṣṭhanti Pādapā:..

7.12 The current time is very difficult for simple and gentlemanly persons. Any clever person with selfish interest easily cheats them. This shloka appropriately deals with such a situation. Through this shloka, Chanakya advises simple and gentlemanly persons that sometimes their simplicity and righteousness can become a curse for them. Their simplicity is exploited by evil and selfish persons. For this, they do not even hesitate to harm them. Citing an example, he says in the forest only the trees, which grow straight are cut and nobody bothers about trees which grow in a haphazard manner. So, a man should not be so simple that people easily exploit him.

Yatrōdakaṃ Tatra Vasanti Hansā: Tathaiva Śuṣkaṃ Parivarjayanti.
Na Hansatulyēna Narēṇa Bhāvyaṃ Punastyajantē Punarāśrayantē..

7.13 In this shloka, comparing the selfish person with a swan, Chanakya says that only when there is water in the pond, the swans stay and build their nests on the bank. But when the pond dries, they break all the attachments and fly away. The selfish person also behaves in the same fashion. Till his vested interest is not fulfilled, he remains with his provider and showers his affection. Once his vested interest is fulfilled, he leaves his provider. So, a man should not be selfish like the swan. If he stays with him in good times, then he should also support with determination in adversity.

Upārjitānāṃ Vittānāṃ Tyāga Ēva Hi Rakṣaṇam.
Taḍāgōdarasaṃsthānāṃ Parivāha Ivāmbhasām..

7.14 Excessive wealth not only corrupts a man's mind but also makes him greedy and selfish. Clarifying this saying, Chanakya says that if in time the still water in a pond is not changed, it rots and becomes useless. In order to retain its usefulness, it should run continuously. Similarly, the amassed wealth must be circulated by donation. This not only earns esteem/respect for a man in this world, it also opens doors for ensuring happiness in the other world.

Yasyārthāstasya Mitrāṇi Yasyārthāstasya Bāndhavā:.
Yasyārthā: Sa Pumām̐llōkē Yasyārthā: Sa Ca Jīvati:..

7.15 The importance, influence and usefulness of wealth has been established for centuries. Even Chanakya accepts that wealth is more important than intelligence and knowledge. Explaining it, he says that even if someone is short on knowledge/wisdom but has unlimited wealth, he will be respected in the society. In contrast, a poor but knowledgeable, intelligent and wise person is looked down upon. The power of wealth is so great that even unfamiliar persons develop relationship, whereas poverty even drives away relations. The paucity of wealth leaves you alone in adversity. It is only wealth which gains man the highest respect in society.

Svargasthitānāmiha Jīvalōkē Catvāri Cihnāni Vasanti Dēhē.
Dānaprasaṅgō Madhurā Ca Vāṇī Dēvārcanaṃ Brāhmaṇatarpaṇaṃ Ca..

7.16 On identifying great persons, Chanakya says that they have the four combined qualities of donating, sweet talk, praying and respecting scholars. He is ever ready to donate; his speech is sweet at all times; his psyche is fully devoted to God and he always respects scholars.

Atyantakōpa: Kaṭukā Ca Vāṇī Daridratā Ca Svajanēṣu Vairam.
Nīcaprasaṅga: Kulahīnasēvā Vihnāni Dēhē Narakasthitānām..

7.17 On identifying the evil persons, Chanakya says that they have extreme anger, they always utter poisonous speech, they are ever ready to cause harm to friends/relations, they keep the company of evil men and they work for contemptible men. Such persons bear extreme hardships of hell, even while living in this world. Poverty and being characterless are their other ill qualities.

Gamyatē Yadi Mṛgēandra-Mandiraṃ Labhyatē Karikapōlamaukitakam.
Jambukālayagatē Ca Prāpyatē Sa Vatsa-Puccha-Khara Carma-Khaṇḍanam..

7.18 On the positive effects of being in the company of great men, Chanakya says the forehead diamond of the elephant could be found in the cave of the lion, but only bones and meat will be found in the abode of the jackal. Similarly, one can learn a lot in the company of gentlemen. Contrarily, the company of evil men will only lead to misdeeds and crime.

Śuna: Pucchamiva Vyarthaṃ Jīvitaṃ Vidyayā Vinā.
Na Guhyagōpanē Śaktaṃ Na Ca Daṃśānivāraṇē..

7.19 Chanakya has stressed on the importance of education. He has compared an illiterate person to a dog's tail. He says that as a dog cannot cover his vitals or get rid of flies/mosquitoes with his tail, similarly, a foolish and illiterate person cannot properly take care or protect his family. So, a man should gain knowledge instead of craving for food and wealth.

Vāca: Śaucaṃ Ca Manasa: Śaucamindriyanigraha:.
Sarvabhūtē Dayā Śaucaṃ Ētacchaucaṃ Parārthinām..

7.20 Having the spirit of looking after the welfare of others and kindness only can purify a person. In the absence of this spirit, purifying your mind, speech or senses has no meaning. Elaborating further, Chanakya says a person taking care of the welfare of others is pure in the true sense. The soul of such person does not get corrupted even in bad company.

Puṣpē Gandhaṃ Tilē Tailaṃ Kāṣṭhērinaṃ Payasi Ghṛtam.
Ikṣau Guḍaṃ Tathā Dēhē Paśyātmānaṃ Vivēkata:..

7.21 Even though flowers have fragrance, seeds have oil, wood burns, milk contains ghee and sugarcane is sweet, all these things are not visible. Similarly, in the case of men, the soul is present in the body but cannot be seen. However, it can be felt by wisdom. So, a man should enlighten it by wisdom.

❑

Chapter 8

Adhamā Dhanamicchanti Dhanaṃ Mānaṃ Ca Madhyamā:.
Uttamā Mānaamicchanti Mānō Hi Mahatāṃ Dhanam..

8.1 According to Chanakya, evil and cruel persons have the lust for wealth. To obtain it, they do not hesitate even to adopt any despicable means. Their sole objective is to get wealthy. Even though middle-income people also consider wealth to be important, but for them, their esteem/respect is also equally important. So, even though they have the lust to become wealthy, they hesitate to adopt despicable means. Whereas for righteous persons, their esteem/respect is most important. So, to retain it, they even refuse the most valuable thing.

Ikṣurāpa: Payō Mūlaṃ Tāmbūlaṃ Phalamauṣadham.
Bhakṣayitvāapi Kartavyā: Snānadānādikā: Kriyā:..

8.2 In this shloka, Chanakya describes the relaxations granted to sick and hungry persons in the scriptures. He says that water, sugarcane, milk, vegetables, beetle leaf, fruits and medicines have been classified as most pure substances in the scriptures. So, they can perform religious rites, even after consuming them. There will be no impediment.

Dīpō Bhakṣayatē Dhvāntaṃ Kajjalaṃ Ca Prasūyatē.
Yadannaṃ Bhakṣayēninatyaṃ Jāyatē Tādṛśī Prajā..

8.3 Chanakya most definitely accepts the fact that good/bad qualities and conduct of the parents' influence their children. He says even though a lamp dispels darkness, its soot is black. Similarly, the type of food a man consumes, his children will like that. Elaborating this, Chanakya says that if a person is a cheat, characterless and evils pirited, then his children will also possess these ill qualities. Against this, a gentleman's children will be intelligent, simple, honest and tolerant. Therefore, a man should always imbibe good qualities.

Vittaṃ Dēhi Guṇānvitēṣu Matimannānyatra Dēhi Kvacit
Prāptaṃ Vārinidhērjalaṃ Ghanamukhē Mādhuryayuktaṃ Sadā.
Jīvān Sthāvarajaṅgamāṃśca Sakalān Sañjīvya Bhūmaṇḍalam
Bhūya: Paśya Tadēva Kōṭiguṇitaṃ Gacchantamambhōnidhim..

8.4 Even though Chanakya has stressed on the obligation to donate, he says that it should not be given to everyone. In this context, he says that as the clouds absorb water from the sea and release it as lifegiving rain over the fields, the same water multiples manifold and merges back into the sea. Similarly, if donation is given to a person who is tolerant, learned, honest and a gentleman, then it is received back a hundred times. However, it should never be given to a person who is lazy, evil, jealous of others, immoral and a sinner, otherwise such a donation will be a waste.

Cāṇḍālānāṃ Sahasrē Ca Sūribhistattvadarśibhi:.
Ēkō Hi Yavana: Prōktō Na Nīcō Yavanātpara:..

8.5 Chanakya cautions that it is in the interest of a man to stay away from the company of a degenerated and evil person. If possible, he should not even come face-to-face with him. In the scriptures also, the Rishi-Munis have compared such persons to a hundred devils. According to him, an evil person is extremely dangerous, degenerated and unfaithful. Merely being in their company can cause several crises and sorrows.

Tailābhyaṅgē Citādhūmē Maithunē Kṣaurakarmaṇi.
Tāvadbhavati Cāṇḍālō Yāvat Snānaṃ Na Cācarēt..

8.6 In the Hindu scriptures, bathing has been described as an important and purifying act. In this context, Chanakya says that after oil massage, visit to the crematorium, mating and shaving, a man's body becomes impure. Bathing is the act which purifies him again, so after the above-cited acts, it is essential to take bath. It is also healthy. However, one must not bathe immediately after mating, as it is not healthy.

Ajīrṇē Bhēṣajaṃ Vāri Jīrṇē Vāri Balapradam.
Bhōjanē Cāmṛtaṃ Vāri Bhōjanāntē Viṣapradam..

8.7 On drinking water, Chanakya says that the stomach is an important organ. It is the stomach which controls your fitness. It is, therefore, essential that a man should keep his digestion in order. In case of indigestion, water acts as a medicine. So, drink a lot of water, but do so before taking food or after digestion of the food. If water is taken immediately after taking food, it acts like slow poison and deteriorates the body.

Hataṃ Jñānaṃ Kriyāhīnaṃ Hataścājñānatō Nara:.
Hataṃ Nirnāyakaṃ Sainyaṃ Striyō Naṣṭā Hyabhartṛkā:..

8.8 If knowledge is not used, it is forgotten; the neglect of a person makes him inactrive; without the commander, the army dissipates and without the husband, the wife is ruined.

Vṛddhakālē Mṛtā Bhāryā Bandhuhastē Gataṃ Dhanam.
Bhōjanaṃ Ca Parādhīnaṃ Tisra: Puṃsāṃ Viḍambanā:..

8.9 Old age has been described as the man's most pathetic and difficult stage of life. At this age, the wife's death, usurping of one's wealth by close relations and being dependent for food—these three things are extremely painful. He says that wife is a true companion in old age and her absence makes a man completely helpless. If a man has wealth in old age, he does not have to be dependent on others for food. So, to avert this pathetic state, a man should save wealth.

Nāgnihōtraṃ Vinā Vēdā Na Ca Dānaṃ Vinā Kriyā.
Na Bhāvēna Vinā Siddhistasmādbhāvō Hi Kāraṇam..

8.10 According to Chanakya, getting the knowledge from the Vedas, without performing yagna/havan is useless. Also if after the yagna, the honorarium is not paid, all the benefits of the yagna are negated. Through these statements, Chanakya wishes to clarify that a man cannot get success in any task, if he does not have full faith in it. In other words, only that task is successful, which is done with mental dedication and sacrifice. So, a man should do all the auspicious and virtuous tasks with full dedication and sacrifice.

Kāṣṭhapāṣāṇadhātūnāṃ Kṛtvā Bhāvēna Sēvanam.
Śraddhayā Ca Tayā Siddhastasya Viṣṇu: Prasīdati..

8.11 It is the practice in the Hindu Dharma to pray before the idols of God made of wood, stone or metal. Chanakya believes that a man can pray before idols of God made of any material, but it is necessary to have true dedication and reverence. In fact, only on account of this faith, God resides in man's heart and he feels the presence of God in inanimate objects and attains salvation.

Na Dēvō Vidyatē Kāṣṭhē Na Pāṣāṇē Na Mṛṇmayē.
Bhāvē Hi Vidyatē Dēvastasmād Bhāvō Hi Kāraṇam..

8.12 Believing in the idols of God made from wood, stone and metal to be the true form of God and praying before them results in God's blessings. In other words, God does not exist in inanimate objects but in your faith. That is why, it is said that you cannot get salvation without dedication and faith.

Śānti Tulyaṃ Tapō Nāsti Na Santōṣātparaṃ Sukham.
Na Tṛṣṇāyā: Parō Vyādhina: Ca Dharmō Dayāpara:..

8.13 Chanakya has written this shloka using his entire life's experience. He says that in this world, there is no greater devotion than peace, greater happiness than contentment and sickness than greed. Likewise feeling for others' sorrows and being ever ready to help are man's true duties. In other words, a man should shun anger and bear all difficulties peacefully. Such actions of a man are comparable to the severe devotions of ascetics. Man should be satisfied with whatever means he possesses. Contentment alone will give him complete happiness whereas sickness like greed will even deprive him of actual happiness. Praying to God and visiting religious places are not the only duties of a man, serving others and humanity are his true duties.

Krōdhō Vaivasvatō Rājā Tṛṣṇā Vaitaraṇī Nadī.
Vidyā Kāmadudhā Dhēnu: Santōṣō Nandanaṃ Vanam..

8.14 Anger completely ruins a person. Anger is the image of the God of death, who is ever ready to grasp the person in its hideous jaws. Under its influence, the person loses his senses and it leads him to perform despicable acts. It is said that in the journey to the other world, on the way is a river named *Vaitarni*. It is very painful for the soul to cross it. Chanakya has compared greed to the *Vaitarni* river and he says that, a man should make all efforts to stay away from greed. He has compared education to the 'Kamdhenu cow' which fulfills all wishes. He says that a man, who learns, is certain to get all his wishes fulfilled. Similarly, Chanakya has compared contentment to Lord Indra's abode, Nandan forest, which is pleasing and charming. So, he has stressed on living in contentment.

Guṇō Bhūṣayatē Rūpaṃ Śīlaṃ Bhūṣayatē Kulam.
Siddhirbhūṣayatē Vidyāṃ Bhōgō Bhūṣayatē Dhanam..

8.15 According to Chanakya, beauty is enhanced by good qualities, whereas the grace of the dynasty lies in morality. The test of your education is through your ability to create wealth and the value of money rises by using it. Elaborating this, Chanakya says that even if you are very beautiful and youthful but without any qualities, then you will face insult and disregard. A person's behaviour decides the superiority of his dynasty. If a man believes in righteousness, then his dynasty will get appropriate respect/ regard in the society. Any learning through which you cannot earn money is useless. If wealth is only amassed and not used, then it loses its importance.

Nirguṇasya Hataṃ Rūpaṃ Du:Śīlasya Hataṃ Kulam.
Asiddhasya Hatā Vidyā Abhōgēna Hataṃ Dhanam..

8.16 Improper behaviour ruins beauty. If you lose your morality, then your dynasty will be defamed. Similarly, without full involvement, you cannot attain success in any task and misuse of money leads to its dissipation.

Śucirbhūmigataṃ Tōyaṃ Śuddhā Nārī Pativratā.
Śuci: Kṣēmakarō Rājā Santōṣī Brāhmaṇa: Śuci:..

8.17 Water stored in the depths of the earth, a loyal woman, a welfare-inclined king and a content Brahmin—Chanakya has called these four utmost pure. According to him, the water stored in the earth contains minerals, so it is healthy. Nobody is as radiant as a loyal woman. Even Gods acknowledge her. A welfare-inclined king is always concerned about the welfare and good of his people. He is considered as a great person. Honorarium paid to a content Brahmin is received back manifold. So, a man must respect everyone.

Asantuṣṭā Dvijā Naṣṭā: Santuṣṭāśca Mahībhṛta:.
Salajjā Gaṇikā Naṣṭā Nirlajjāśca Kulāṅganā:..

8.18 A discontented Brahmin, an unambitious contented king, a shameful prostitute and a shameless status woman—Chanakya has called these four to be extremely damaging for a man. He says that a discontented Brahmin can never earn respect in the society. An unambitious king can never be concerned about the welfare and progress of his people. As a result, pretty soon his enemies ruin his kingdom. Any shameful prostitute can never satisfy her clients. As a result, they shun her and in the end, she dies of hunger. In contrast, a shameless status woman falls in bad company and ruins herself and her family.

Kiṃ Kulēna Viśālēna Vidyāhīnēna Dēhinām.
Duṣkulīnōpi Vidvāṃśca Dēvairapi Supūjyatē..

8.19 In this shloka, Chanakya enlightens on the importance of learning. He emphatically says that in the absence of learning and good qualities, even a person born in an upper caste is mocked. Against this, a person born in lower caste with learning and good qualities, attains status in the society. In other words, it is not enough to be born in an upper caste to attain greatness. It is necessary for him to be tolerant, patient, learned and welfare minded.

Vidvān Praśasyatē Lōkē Vidvān Gacchati Gauravam.
Vidyayā Labhyatē Sarvaṃ Vidyā Sarvatra Pūjyatē..

8.20 Explaining the importance of education, Chanakya says that only scholars are praised everywhere; they get fame/respect from every place. They get all the happiness because of education. In fact, all over the world, education is worshipped; nothing is more valuable. Therefore, a person under them is also respected in the society. So, a man must get educated. This will open the doors of progress for him.

Māṃsabhakṣai: Surāpānairmūrkhaiścākṣaravarjitai:.
Paśubhi: Puruṣākārairbhārākrāntā Ca Mēdinī..

8.21 Chanakya has compared men who eat meat, drink liquor, are foolish or are illiterate, to animals. He says such men behave like animals. They do not contribute anything to society and state, but bad qualities. You cannot expect welfare or gentlemanly behaviour from them. They are only excessive weight on the earth. Their life is a waste.

Annahīnō Dahēd Rāṣṭraṃ Mantrahīnaśca Ṛtvija:.
Yajamānaṃ Dānahīnō Nāsti Yajñasamō Ripu:..

8.22 In Hindu scriptures, performing yagya/havan, on auspicious occasions has been considered very important. Lord Brahma has compared it to the kalpavriksha which fulfills all the wishes of a man. This saying has been accepted by Chanakya also. But he argues that if while performing the yagna there is deficiency of any kind in its ceremony/arrangement, then its effects can turn negative/causing difficulties. So, while performing the yagna grains should be donated, the hymns should be recited according to procedure and the priests should be given proper honorarium. If this does not happen then the yagna can cause ruin. So, yagna should only be performed when the capability to perform it as per the correct procedures exists.

❑

Chapter 9

Mukitamicchasi Cittāta Viṣayān Viṣavat Tyaja.
Kṣamārjavaṃ Dayā Śaucaṃ Satyaṃ Pīyūṣavad Bhaja..

9.1 In this shloka, Chanakya preaches willing persons, the ways to attain salvation. He says that if a man wants release from the cycle of life-death and attain salvation, then he should completely abandon perversions like sex, anger, greed, allurement and arrogance. These perversions are like poison for man. Under their influence, a man remains tied to affection/wealth for life. Instead of these perversions, a man should imbibe qualities like forgiveness, simplicity, patience, politeness, honesty, generosity, welfare, mercy, truth, love and purity. This enables him to be free of all sinful acts and attain salvation.

Parasparasya Marmāṇi Yē Bhāṣantē Narādhamā:.
Ta Ēva Vilayaṃ Yānti Valmīkōdarasarpavat..

9.2 Persons who expose others secrets, Chanakya has called them degenerated, meddlesome and evil. He says that such persons initially feel elated by insulting one or the other, later they are ruined like a snake trapped in an ant hill. People should stay away from them.

Gandha: Suvarṇē Phalamikṣudaṇḍē Nākāri Puṣpaṃ Khalu Candanasya.
Vidvān Dhanāḍhyaśca Nṛpaściāyu: Dhātu: Purā Kōpi Na Buddhidōbhūt..

9.3 Like gold does not have fragrance, sugarcane is not a fruit and sandalwood does not flower, similarly, scholars are not wealthy nor do the kings have long life. The creator of the universe did what he thought best. Had he taken care of the above-cited deficiencies, then it would have been much better for the world. But a change in any manner in the universe's laws is not possible.

Sarvauṣadhīnāmamṛtā Pradhānā Sarvēṣu Saukhyēṣvaśanaṃ Pradhānam.
Sarvēndriyāṇāṃ Nayanaṃ Pradhānaṃ Sarvēṣu Gātrēṣu Śira: Pradhānam..

9.4 In this shloka, Chanakya clarifies that there is no medicine as pure and life bestower as nectar. It cures all ailments. So, in medicines, nectar is most superior. Eyes are the most important senses amongst all the senses. Through these a man is able to see the God's beautiful creation. In their absence, life is filled with darkness. Likewise, the brain controls the man's body, without it, the body is useless.

Dūtō Na Sañcarati Khē Na Calēcca Vārnttā
Pūrvaṃ Na Jalpitamidaṃ Na Ca Saṅgamōsti.
Vyōmnia Sthitaṃ Raviśaśigrahaṇaṃ Praśastaṃ
Jānāti Yō Dvijavara: Sa Kathaṃ Na Vidvān.

9.5 According to Chanakya, those who discovered the solar and lunar eclipse are also called scholars. For this, they didn't send any emissary in space nor discussed it with anyone. They studied the facts of the space, researched them and gained all the knowledge, staying on the earth itself. This clearly shows that scholars are able to understand the inner thoughts of others without saying anything. Nothing remains a secret in front of their intelligence and knowledge.

Vidyārthī Sēvaka: Pāntha: Kṣudhārtō Bhayakātara:.
Bhāṇḍārī Pratīhārī Ca Sapta Suptān Prabōdhayēt..

9.6 A student, employee, traveller, hungry person, scared person, storekeeper and doorman—can only complete their tasks while remaining awake.

So, Chanakya says that if you find them sleeping, awaken them. On awakening, the student can complete his studies and the employee will be able to complete his task on time. Likewise on awakening the traveller, he will be able to protect his wealth, as well as will be able to reach his destination quickly. After awakening, feed the hungry and reassure the scared. The job of the storekeeper is to protect the store and the guard to police the house while remaining awake. If they sleep, then thieves and dacoits will rule the roost. So, they also must be awakened.

Ahiṃ Nṛpaṃ Ca Śārdūlaṃ Kiaṭiṃ Ca Bālakaṃ Tathā.
Paraśvānaṃ Ca Mūrkhaṃ Ca Supta Suptān Na Bōdhayēt..

9.7 In the above shloka, Chanakya has talked about awakening certain people. In this shloka, he prohibits awakening some living beings. He says not to awaken a snake, king, lion, wild boar, child, fool, honebee and other's dog, otherwise he will face great hardships. These beings are better off sleeping.

Arthāadhītāśca Yairvēdāstathā Śūdrānnabhōjinā:.
Tē Dvijā: Kiṃ Kariṣyanti Nirviṣā Iva Pannagā:..

9.8 Chanakya has called a Brahmin who only uses his knowledge to earn wealth, useless for the society. His being or not being in the society is of no consequence. He will never be known for his intelligence and knowledge in the world.

Yasmin Ruṣṭē Bhayaṃ Nāsti Tuṣṭē Dhanāgama:.
Nigrahōnugrahō Nāsti Sa Ruṣṭa: Kiṃ Kariṣyati..

9.9 Any person, whose anger has no impact and his happiness does not benefit anyone, such a person's behaviour cannot influence anyone. You should not expect any sympathy or favour from such a person. This person only exists for himself and he is not concerned with anyone else.

Nirviṣēṇāpi Sarpēṇa Kartavyā Mahatī Phaṇā.
Viṣamastu Na Cāpyastu Ghaṭāṭōpō Bhayaṅkara..

9.10 In this shloka, Chanakya displays his diplomatic prowess. Approving showmanship of strength and influence, he says that like people are scared of a hissing snake, even though he may not be poisonous, similarly, a person without any influence must create influence in the society by showmanship. People may not be aware that the snake is not poisonous; similarly, people are scared of showmanship. In such a situation, the person is never mocked.

Prātardyūtaprasaṅgēna Madhyāhnē Strīsapraṅgata.
Rātrau Cauryaprasaṅgēna Kālō Gacchatyadhīmatām..

9.11 Discussing the daily activities of a fool and an intelligent person, Chanakya says that a fool's day starts with gambling. In the afternoon, they mate and their nights are spent in robbing or other sinful activities. Against this a gentleman's, and intelligent person's day starts with good deeds and the whole day is spent in other's welfare. So, a man should use his time purposefully like a gentleman.

Svahastagrathitā Mālā Svahastaghṛṣṭacandanam.
Svahastalikhitaṃ Stōtraṃ Śakrasyāpi Śriyaṃ Harēt..

9.12 On performing religious ceremonies, Chanakya says that a man can reap the benefits of pleasing the God, if he performs all the religious ceremonies himself. Making the flower garland and placing on the Gods idol himself, applying the self-made sandalwood paste and reciting the self-written hymns in the praise of God, etc. will enable him to obtain God's grace. In contrast, if he gets all these ceremonies done through a servant, then the benefits will accrue to the servant. So, a man should perform all the religious ceremonies himself.

Ikṣudaṇḍāstilā: Kṣudrā: Kāntā Hēma Ca Mēdinī.
Candanaṃ Dadhi Tāmbūlaṃ Mardanaṃ Guṇavardhanam..

9.13 The more you subject to pressure the sugarcane, oilseeds, *shudra* (person of the lowest caste), woman, gold, earth, sandalwood, curd and betel leaf, the more qualities they develop. The more you crush sugarcane and oilseeds you will get more juice and oil. The tougher stand you take to educate a *shudra* and a woman, the more quickly they will learn. The more intensely gold is heated, the more it shines and becomes purer. The better the earth is ploughed, the better is the yield. Similarly, the more you rub sandalwood, curd and betel leaf, the more you enhance their qualities.

Daridratā Dhīratayā Virājatē Kuvastratā Śubhratayā Virājatē.
Kadannatā Cōṣṇatayā Virājatē Kurūpatā Śīlatayā Virājatē..

9.14 Chanakya says that you must be satisfied with whatever you have. A poor man should be patient. This will enable him to endure the difficulties of his poverty, with his limited resources. Even if he keeps his cheap clothes neat and clean, he will be able to improve his appearance. Even if he eats his frugal food hot, it will be tasty. Similarly, if a wise and intelligent person is ugly looking, he will not face impediments. So, a man should look for ways to be happy and satisfied, even in the above-cited circumstances.

❑

Chapter 10

Dhanahīnō Na Hīnaśca Dhanika: Sa Suniścaya:.
Vidyāratnēna Yō Hīna: Sa Hīna: Sarvavastuṣu..

10.1 According to Chanakya, no wealth is greater than education. Accepting this important fact, he says that a person without wealth is not poor, but a person without wisdom and education, is truly poor. Even a fool can earn wealth, but only a few fortunate get educated. A wealthy fool cannot earn respect/repute for himself. However, a poor scholar can attain a respectable place in the society. Therefore, getting educated has more value than earning wealth, so a man should always make efforts for gaining it.

Dṛṣṭipūtaṃ Nyasēt Pādaṃ Vastrapūtaṃ Pibējjalam.
Śāstrapūtaṃ Vadēd Vākya Mana: Pūtaṃ Samācarēt..

10.2 Through this shloka, Chanakya has cautioned man to act only after due consideration; like drinking water after filtering it through a cloth sieve. That is, he should talk in a sweet tone and behave politely with everyone. That will ensure that he never stumbles and faces defeat in life. Clarifying, Chanakya says that a man's behaviour is enough to make people bow before him. Even enemies can be won over.

Sukhārthī Cēt Tyajēt Vidyāṃ Vidyārthī Ca Tyajēt Sukham.
Sukhārthina: Kutō Vidyā Kutō Vidyārthina: Sukham..

10.3 According to Chanakya, there are lot of obstacles and difficulties in getting education. So, the students, who desire pleasure, should shun the idea of getting education. The paths to enjoying physical pleasure and getting education are separate. To attain both simultaneously is impossible. Whereas, on one hand, physical pleasure is pleasing and delightful, on the other hand, getting education is like performing a severe religious austerity. To obtain it, one needs to do self-mortification like gold is heated. So, one must choose only one, with due consideration.

Kavaya: Kiṃ Na Paśyanti Kiṃ Na Kurvanti Yōṣita:.
Madyapā: Kiṃ Na Jalpanti Kiṃ Na Bhakṣanti Vāyasā:..

10.4 Chanakya says that a poet's imagination is limitless, it is impossible to fathom it by an average person. It is beyond anyone to enter the palace of his imagination. Likewise, men are unaware of the true power of women. It is difficult to imagine what a woman can do if she becomes obstinate. A drunkard loses control over his speech. So, it is difficult to predict how he will behave. Even the crow does not know what he should eat or what he should not eat. In other words, it is not possible to know any living beings' limit. In times of crisis, a man can cross any limits.

Raṅkaṃ Karōti Rājānaṃ Rājānaṃ Raṅkamēva Ca.
Dhaninaṃ Nirdhanaṃ Caiva Nirdhanaṃ Dhaninaṃ Vidhi:..

10.5 Extolling the supremacy of fate, Chanakya says that it is impossible for anyone to overrule it. It is the miracle of fate which can make a king to become a pauper and a pauper to become a king. Whatever God has in store for a man, he has to bear the consequences accordingly. The fate cannot be altered in any manner. Consequently, certain events can occur in a man's life, which no one can predict. So, as far as possible a man should perform good deeds. His forbidding cannot be dispelled, but its impact can be minimised.

Lubdhānāṃ Yācaka: Śatrurmūrkhāṇāṃ Bōdhaka: Ripu:.
Jārastrīṇāṃ Pati: Śatruścōrāṇāṃ Candramā Ripu:..

10.6 It really hurts a greedy person to give money, so he considers anyone who asks for alms, charity or donation as his enemy. Likewise, a knowledgeable preacher cuts short a fool and tries to instill knowledge in a him. So, a fool considers him as his enemy. For a disloyal wife, her husband is like an enemy, because he tries to restrict her independence. The thieves find it difficult to burgle in a moonlit night, so they consider it their enemy. In other words, through this shloka, Chanakya clarifies that evil persons consider everyone who follows the path of righteousness, as their enemy; yet gentlemen continue on their righteous paths.

Anta:Sāravihīnānāmupadēśō Na Jāyatē.
Malayācalasaṃsargāt Na Vēṇuścandanāyatē..

10.7 As the bamboos inspite of being surrounded by sandalwood trees, growing on Malyachal Mountain, are not as fragrant as them, do not develop the characteristics of sandalwood, similarly, a fool in the company of scholars cannot become a scholar. Explaining this, Chanakya says that a person who does not have the ability to think/understand, who is not eager to learn, cannot be taught inspite of best efforts. Any preaching to such persons is a waste. For that, a man should be curious.

Yasya Nāsti Svayaṃ Prajñā Śāstraṃ Tasya Karōti Kim.
Lōcanābhyāṃ Vihīnasya Darpaṇa: Kiṃ Kariṣyati..

10.8 Chanakya says that mirror was made for people having vision. They can see themselves in it. But for the blind, it serves no purpose. You cannot blame the mirror for it. Similarly, the Vedas/scriptures were created and for intelligent and wise people. They are beneficial only for people, who have thinking and understanding ability. Fools cannot benefit from them.

Durjanaṃ Sajjanaṃ Kartumupāyō Na Hi Bhūtalē.
Apānaṃ Śatadhā Dhautaṃ Na Śrēṣṭhamindriyaṃ Bhavēt.

10.9 Explaining the nature of an evil person, Chanakya says that as by repeated washing, your excreting parts cannot be cleansed, similarly, even by numerous preaching of wisdom, the nature of the evil person cannot be changed. All efforts to reform them fail.

Āptadvēṣād Bhavēnmṛtyu: Paradvēṣād Dhanakṣaya:.
Rājadvēṣād Bhavēnnāśō Brahmadvēṣātkulakṣaya:..

10.10 In this shloka, Chanakya has cited the consequences of envy. He says that the person, who is envious of saints, soon meets his death. Being envious of your enemy results in death and loss of wealth. Being envious of the king results in death, loss of wealth and respect. Likewise, being envious of the Brahmin results in death-loss of wealth-respect, along with ruin of his entire family. So, a man should always get the blessings from gentlemen. His blessings will enhance his wealth and bring prosperity for his family. He will also live long and enjoy all the pleasures of life.

Varaṃ Vanaṃ Vyāghragajēndrasēvitaṃ Drumālaya: Patraphalāmbubhōjanam.
Tṛṇēṣu Śayyā Śatajīrṇavalkalaṃ Na Bandhumadhyē Dhanahīna Jīvanam..

10.11 Through this shloka, Chanakya has called that a wise person, who on becoming poor, instead of staying with his relations, prefers to stay in the forest amidst wild animals like lion, elephant, tiger, etc. in a tree house, eats fruits and roots, drinks water, sleeps on a grass mattress and covers himself with leaves. Explaining this, Chanakya says that on becoming poor, a person may be mocked on several occasions. Such a situation is extremely stressful and can cause mental tension. Nobody supports him when he becomes poor. So, it is wise to leave and stay in the forest.

Viprō Vakṣastasya Mūlaṃ Ca Sandhyā Vēdā: Śākhā Dharmakarmāṇi Patram.
Tasmānmūlaṃ Yatnatō Rakṣaṇīyaṃ Chinnē Mūlē Naiva Śākhā Na Patram..

10.12 Giving a form to the imaginary eternal tree, Chanakya says that the Brahmin is eternal tree on the earth. Prayers are its roots and Vedas its branches. Religious ceremonies are its beautiful leaves growing on the branches. He says that roots of the tree are most important, as the tree survives on the roots. If the roots weaken or die, its does not take long for the tree to dry. So, the root must be duly protected.

Mātā Ca Kamalādēvī Pitā Dēvō Janārdana:.
Bāndhavā Viṣṇubhaktāśca Svadēśō Bhuvanatrayam..

10.13 In this shloka, Chanakya says that anyone whose mother is Goddess Lakshmi, father is Lord Vishnu and the worshippers are classified as his relations, such a person is most superior. For him, all the three worlds are like his country—it is as if he owns all the three worlds. But to attain such a state, a man should possess the qualities of gentlemanliness, benevolence, tolerance and charity.

Ēkavṛkṣasamārūḍhā Nānā Varṇā: Vihaṅgamā:.
Prabhātē Dikṣu Daśasu Kā Tatra aparidēvanā..

10.14 Chanakya has explained the concept of life and death in a very simplistic manner. He says that a crow, pigeon, sparrow and parrot—even though being of different species and colour, sleep on the same tree in the night. But at the crack of dawn, they all fly away to their own destinations. Similarly, the human souls also settle for some time in families, in the form of trees. Then at the appointed hour, they fly away from that tree. So, one should not grieve or feel sorrow on their departure. This is the law of the nature and the entire universe is guided by it. Even the creator of this world, Lord Brahma cannot change it.

Buddhiryasya Balaṃ Tasya Nirbuddhēśca Kutō Balam.
Vanē Siṃhō Madōnmatta: Śaśakēna Nipātita:..

10.15 Chanakya says that in the hour of need, only the intelligent man can effectively use his strength. Even though it might be less, his strength is significant. Contrarily, a fool's strength may be immense but it is useless, as in the absence of intelligence, he will never be able to use it effectively. So, it is more important to have intelligence rather than more or less strength. It is only using his intelligence a rabbit killed a lion, by making him jump into the well.

Kā Cintā Mama Jīvanē Yadi Harirviśvambharō Gīyatē
Nō Cēdarbhakajīvanāya Jananīstanyaṃ Kathaṃ Nirmayēt.
Ityālōcya Muhurmuhuryadupatē Lakṣmīpatē Kēvalaṃ
Tvatpādāmbujasēvanēna Satataṃ Kālō Mayā Nīyatē..

10.16 Through this shloka praying before Lord Vishnu, Chanakya says that it is only Lord Vishnu who provides food to the whole world. So, he is called the provider. Had he not been the provider, there would be no milk in the breasts of a mother, at the time of birth of the child. Oh Shri Vishnu! Oh Lord! For your greatness, I, Chanakya, bow before you and fold my hands a thousand times. But here Chanakya also clarifies that even though man should have full faith in God, he should not shy away from his efforts. God will fulfil his wishes, only if he also makes the effort.

Annāddaśaguṇaṃ Piṣṭaṃ Piṣṭāddaśaguṇaṃ Paya:.
Payasōaṣṭaguṇaṃ Māṃsaṃ Māṃsāddaśaguṇaṃ Ghṛtam..

10.17 In this shloka, Chanakya has expressed his desire to learn and understand other languages in addition to Sanskrit. He says that even after drinking nectar, the Gods impatiently desire to kiss the Apsaras, similarly even after entirely learning the Sanskrit language, I have the yearning to learn the other superior languages of the world, because after learning these languages, I will attain the due respect/honour in the world. This shloka of Chanakya aptly applies in the present times.

Gīrvāṇavāṇīṣu Viśiṣṭabuddhistathāpi Bhāṣāntaralōlupōham.
Yathā Surāṇāmamṛtē Sthitēpi Svargāṅganānāmadharāsavē Ruci:..

10.18 According to Chanakya, the addition of *ghee* in the food provides maximum strength and nourishment. He says that in comparison to wheat, its flour provides ten times more strength. Milk contains ten times more strength than flour. Meat provides eight times more strength than milk. But *ghee* is the best. Its regular intake provides immense strength. So, it must be consumed in the right measure in food.

Śākēna Rōgā Vardhantē Payasā Vardhatē Tanu:.
Ghṛtēna Vardhatē Vīryaṃ Māṃsānmāṃsaṃ Pravardhatē..

10.19 On food products, Chanakya says that excessive consumption of vegetables, etc. invites diseases, whereas milk helps in the development of the body. *Ghee* enhances strength and sperm; meat deposits fat. So, man should consume more milk and *ghee* as compared to vegetables and meat. Against it, consumption of vegetables and meat will deform the body.

❑

Chapter 11

Dātṛtvaṃ Priyavaktṛtvaṃ Dhīratvamucitajñatā.
Abhyāsēna Na Labhyantē Catvāra: Sahajā Guṇā:..

11.1 Chanakya has included charitable nature, sweet talk, patience and the knowledge of right-wrong amongst the superior traits. But he says that man is born with these traits. When a child is born, these traits are present in him instinctively. It is impossible for a person to develop them by practice.

Ātmavargaṃ Parityajya Paravargaṃ Samāśrayēt.
Svayamēva Layaṃ Yāti Yathā Rājānyadharmata:..

11.2 Man's relations are truly his supporters. If he leaves them and rushes towards others, he is ruined very soon, like a king is ruined on account of his unholy behaviour. He clarifies that like the king, who turns away from his religion, is definitely ruined, any person, who gives up his religion and is attracted towards another religion, inspite of being affluent, is ruined. So, a man should never be indifferent to his religion.

Hastī Sthūlatanu: Sa Cāṅkuśavaśa: Kiṃ Hastimātrōṅkuśō
Dīpō Prajvalitē Praṇaśyati Tama: Kiṃ Dīpamātraṃ Tama:.
Vajrēṇāpi Hatā: Patanti Giraya: Kiṃ Vajramātrō Girim
Tējō Yasya Virājatē Sa Balavān Sthūlēṣu Ka: Pratyaya:..

11.3 Through this shloka, Chanakya has proved the superiority of wisdom, cleverness, radiance and strength over size. He says that a huge elephant is controlled by a small iron hook; a lamp's small flame dispels darkness; a hammer can break huge mountains. In other words, a man who is wise, clever, radiant and strong, can overcome even the most difficult problems. The superiority is not in size but inherent in these four qualities.

Kalau Daśasahasrēṣu Haristyajati Mēdinīm.
Tadarthaṃ Jāhnavītōyaṃ Tadarthaṃ Grāmadēvatā..

11.4 It is told in the scriptures that after the completion of the Dark Age, the period of total destruction will commence. In the final destruction, the earth and the universe will be submerged under water. Explaining the signs before the final destruction, he says that ten thousand years before the end of the Dark Age, Lord Vishnu will depart from the earth. Five thousand years earlier, river *Ganges* will disappear from the earth. Two thousand five hundred years earlier, the local Lord will depart from the earth. Like this in the Dark Age when the earth is left with sinners, unholy and cruel persons, then God will depart from the earth.

Gṛhāsaktasya Nō Vidyā Nō Dayā Māṃsabhōjina:.
Dravyalubdhasya Nō Satyaṃ Strainasya Na Pavitratā..

11.5 According to Chanakya, the students, who wish to attain knowledge while being attached to allurement/wealth and pleasures of life, never succeed in their mission. In reality, they are the stumbling blocks to attaining knowledge. By eating a meat man becomes vindictive. In such a state, he loses the virtues of sympathy, welfare, patience and contentment. It is foolish to expect any sympathy from him. Do not expect truthful conduct from a person, who is greedy for money. To earn money, he will resort to telling any kind of lies. Similarly, a person, who is sex-minded, is unmindful of the meaning and importance of purity. Such a person only promotes infidelity.

Na Durjana: Sādhuḍaśāmupauti Bahuprakārairapi Śikṣyamāṇa:.
Āmūlasikta: Payasā Ghṛtēna Na Nimbavṛkṣō Madhuratvamēti..

11.6. An evil and cruel person's behaviour changes mysteriously according to circumstances. So, it is impossible for anyone to understand it. Explaining this, Chanakya says that like the *Neem* tree (Indian lilac), even if it is irrigated with *ghee*, milk and sugar, it does not change its nature, i.e. of bitterness; likewise, even after several preaching and affectionate treatment, it is impossible to turn an evil person into a gentleman. A man's behaviour is dependent on his traits at birth, which have been ordained by Lord Brahma. He behaves accordingly, so a gentleman should not waste his time to reform him.

Antargatamalō Duṣṭastīrthasnānaśatairapi.
Na Śudhyati Yathā Bhāṇḍaṃ Surāyā Dāhitaṃ Ca Sat..

11.7 Chanakya considers the purity of mind over the purity of body. In this context, he says that if a man's thoughts are filled with sins and impurities, then even after taking several dips in religious places, his soul cannot be purified. Like even after putting a liquor container through fire, it does not lose the smell, similarly, even after taking bath in holy water, a man's impurities are not washed away. So, according to Chanakya, a man should purify his mind rather than his body. His welfare lies in it.

Nē Vētti Yō Yasya Guṇaprakarṣaṃ Sa Taṃ Sadā Nindati Nātra Citram.
Yathā Kirātī Karikumbhajātā Muktā: Parityajya Bibharti Guñjā:..

11.8 On a cruel person criticising and insulting a talented and decent person, Chanakya says that if a fool considers a diamond to be an ordinary stone, the diamond cannot be blamed, for it will still remain a diamond. In other words, a cruel person may go to any extent in criticising and humiliating, the talented person's qualities remain as it is, their importance is not diminished. In this circumstance, Chanakya has compared the cruel person to a 'Bhilni' (a mountain tribe female), who considers an elephant's head diamond useless and throws it; and is happy to don a 'Ratti' (seed of Abrus precatorius) necklace. In other words, a person, who criticises a scholar and talented person, is called a fool.

Yastu Saṃvatsaraṃ Pūrṇaṃ Nityaṃ Maunēna Bhuñjati.
Yugakōṭisahasraṃ Tu Svargalōkē Mahīyatē..

11.9 Chanakya says that one must remain silent while eating food. Clarifying its importance, Chanakya says that a person, who observes silence for a year while eating food, enjoys the pleasures of heaven for millions of years. Even Gods also worship him.

Kāmaṃ Krōdhaṃ Tathā Lōbhaṃ Svādaṃ Śṛṅgārakautukē.
Atinidrātisēvē Ca Vidyārthī Hyaṣṭa Varjayēt..

11.10 Chanakya has compared getting education equivalent to doing a 'tap' (rigorous religious austerity). Like the hermit purifies himself in the fire of the religious austerity and earns holy virtues, similarly, a student, while treading on a tortuous path, attains invaluable wealth like education. But weaknesses like sexual desire, anger, greed, allurement, arrogance, taste, makeup, curiosity, excessive sleep and excessive service are its obstacles. So, he should stay away from these and only then he will succeed in getting education.

Akṛṣṭaphalamūlēna Vanāvāsarata: Sadā.
Kurutēharaha: Śrāddhamūṣirvipra: Sa Ucyatē..

11.11 According to Chanakya, only those Brahmins can be classified as Sages, who survive on tuber roots-tree tuber-fruits, etc. consider it superior to live in the forest and pray everyday with offerings for the departed souls. Clarifying this, Chanakya says that a person, who is satisfied with the available means and devotes himself in the worship of God regularly, is a gentleman. Contrary to this, persons, who are greedy, discontented and atheist, are evil.

Ēkāhārēṇa Santuṣṭa: Ṣaṭkarmanirata: Sadā.
Ṛtukālābhigāmī Ca Sa Viprō Dvija Ucyatē..

11.12 In this shloka, Chanakya has described regulations of Brahmin/Dharma. Describing his activities, he says a Brahmin should consume food only once in a day and be satisfied with it. Most of his day should be spent in Yagna-Havan and study of the Vedas. Simultaneously, he should have the quality to donate generously and accept honorarium. Apart from this, he should be able to control delinquencies and mate at the proper time, only for the purpose of producing an offspring. Any person, who observes these as prescribed can only be truly called a Brahmin.

Laikikē Karmaṇi Rata: Paśūnāṃ Paripālaka:.
Vāṇijyakṛṣikartā Sa: Sa Viprō Vaiśya Ucyatē..

11.13 Vedas specify four classes of people. They have been classified based on their profession rather than on their descent or caste. Chanakya says that 'Vaishya' (trader) is a person, who is involved in conventional activities like husbandry, farming and business, etc. If a person born in a Brahmin family undertakes these activities, then he should also be considered a 'Vaishya'.

Lākṣāditailanīlānāṃ Kusumbhamadhusarpiṣām.
Vikrētā Madyamāṃsānāṃ Sa Vipra: Śudra Ucyatē..

11.14 Chanakya says that a person, who is involved in the businesses of lac, oil, ultramarine blue, dyeing colours, honey, *ghee*, liquor and meat, etc. is called a 'Shudhra' (person of the lowest caste). According to him, if a person born in a Brahmin, Kshatriya, or Vaishya family does these jobs, then he should also be considered a Shudhra.

Parakāryavihantā Ca Dāmbhika: Svārthasādhaka:.
Chalī Dvēṣī Mṛdu: Krūrō Viprō Mājārra Ucyatē..

11.15 Any person, who creates obstacles in others good deeds, who misguides to cheat by deceit/fraud and whose atrocities afflict people, such a cruel person, inspite of being a Brahmin, is called a beast. Categorically, a person indulging in degenerated and filthy activities is classified as a beast, even though he might be related to a Brahmin family.

Vāpī-Kūpa-Taḍāgānāmārāma-Sura-Vēśmanām.
Ucchēdanē Nirāśaṅka: Sa Viprō Mlēccha Ucyatē..

11.16 Chanakya has branded a person a barbarian, who feels elated in damaging wells, gardens and temples. According to him, a scholar unconcerned with welfare of the society and his social responsibilities is called a degenerate.

Dēvadravyaṃ Gurudravyaṃ Paradārābhimarśanam.
Nirvāha: Sarvabhūtēṣu Vipraścāṇḍāla Ucyatē..

11.17 A person, who steals the wealth of saints/gurus, who is a consumed adulterator and who has no hesitation in begging for his food, such a person may be a Brahmin but is classified as a hangman. Even though born in an upper caste, they are called degenerates and are looked down in the society.

Dēyaṃ Bhōjyadhanaṃ Sadā Sukṛtirbhinō Sancitavyaṃ Kadā
Śrīkarṇasya Balēśca Vikramapatēradyāpi Kīrti: Sthitā.
Asmākaṃ Madhu Dānabhōgarahitaṃ Naṣṭaṃ Cirāt Sacintam
Nirvāṇāditi Pāṇipādayugalē Gharṣantyahō Makṣikā:..

11.18 Preaching through this shloka, Chanakya says that a king and a gentleman should use their wealth for welfare and donation, instead of amassing it. Practising this, great donor Karna, demon king the Bali and King Vikramaditya earned worldwide fame. Even today their fame is intact. Against this, even the unextracted bee honey is spoiled. Explaining this, Chanakya says that even though a man should save, he should also keep donating. By doing this, while on one hand, he earns respect/honour, on the other hand, he enjoys unrestricted pleasures in the other world.

❑

Chapter 12

Sānandaṃ Sadanaṃ Sutāśca Sudhaya: Kāntā Priyalāpinī
Icchāpūrtidhanaṃ Sanmitraṃ Svayōṣiti Rati: Svājñāparā: Sēvakā:.
Ātithyaṃ Śivapūjanaṃ Pratidinaṃ Miṣṭānnapānaṃ Gṛhē
Sādhō: Saṅgamupāsatē Ca Satataṃ Dhanyō Gṛhasthāśrama:..

12.1 In this shloka, Chanakya describes a happy family man. He says that a man can be said to be happy, if he and his family members are filled with happiness. Where there is all-round happiness and pleasure, the wife has a sweet nature and is loyal, the children are intelligent and well educated; sufficient funds are available, the servants are obedient and loyal; where the guests are appropriately welcomed and looked after, God's worship is practised and saints are welcomed—such a home is filled with happiness. People residing in such a heavenly abode are very lucky.

Ārtēṣu Viprēṣu Dayānvitaśca Yat Śraddhayā Svalpamupaiti Dānam.
Anantapāraṃ Samupaiti Rājan Yaddīyatē Tanna Labhēd Dvijēbhya:..

12.2 On the miracles of donation, Chanakya says a donation is never wasted. In fact, the donated amount is received back ten-fold. So, a man should donate as much as he can to the needy and Brahmins in difficulty. By doing this, his donation opens doors for him to get more wealth.

Dākṣiṇyaṃ Svajanē Dayā Parajanē Śāṭhyaṃ Sadā Durjanē
Prīti: Sādhujanē Sma: Khalajanē Vidvajjanē Cārjavam.
Śauryaṃ Śatrujanē Kṣamā Gurujanē Nārījanē Dhūrtatā
Ityaṃ Yē Puruṣā: Kalāsu Kuśalāstēṣvēva Lōkasthiti:..

12.3 On public dealings, Chanakya says that man should be expert in public dealings. This will ensure that he is always happy. Public dealings cover polite dealing with servants, affectionate dealing with relations and a tough stand with evil persons. In addition, it covers an affectionate and gentle behaviour towards gentlemen and scholars a courageous stand against enemies, an enduring and respectful behaviour towards teachers and witty behaviour towards women. Anyone following these will lead a happy life in the society.

Hastō Dānavivarjitau Śrutipuṭau Sārasvatadrōhiṇau
Nētrē Sādhuvilōkanēna Rahitē Pādau Na Tīrthaṃ Gatau.
Anyāyārjitavittapūrṇamudaraṃ Garvēṇa Tuṅgaṃ Śirō
Rē Rē Jambuka Muñca Muñca Sahasā Nīcaṃ Sunindyaṃ Vapu:..

12.4 In this shloka, Chanakya has defined degenerate and selfish persons. He says that those persons, who refrain from donating, who think that the study of the Vedas is a waste, who consider visiting saints/ascetics is pointless, who have never visited religious places, who have amassed immoral wealth, who remain behind the facade of arrogance and vanity, are degenerate, evil and selfish. They only live for themselves and are not concerned with others. Addressing such persons, Chanakya says that their life is worthless. They are only dead weight on this earth. They are better dead than alive. They should relinquish their life at the earliest, otherwise they will only promote sin and wrong doings.

Patraṃ Naiva Yadā Karīraviṭapē Dōṣō Vasantasya Kiṃ
Nōlūkōpyavalōkatē Yadi Divā Sūryasya Kiṃ Dūṣaṇam.
Varṣā Naiva Paatanti Cātakamukhē Mēghasya Kiṃ Dūṣaṇam
Yatparvūṃ Vidhinā Lalāṭalikhitaṃ Tanmārjituṃ Ka: Kṣama:..

12.5 Chanakya says that it is impossible to change what God has destined in one's fate. In his lifetime, a man acts and reaps accordingly. If the kareel bush does not bloom in spring, then it is no fault of spring; if the owl cannot see in daytime, it is useless to blame the sun; if the rain drops do not fall in the cuckoos mouth, then it is no fault of the clouds. Similarly, the difficulties and hardships which a man bears during his life, are no fault of his. These are pre-destined.

Satsaṅgād Bhavati Hi Sādhutā Khalānāṃ
Sādhūnāṃ Na Hi Khalasaṅgamāt Khalatvam.
Āmōdaṃ Kusuma-Bhavaṃ Mṛdēva Dhattē
Mṛdgandhaṃ Na Hi akusumāni Dhārayanti..

12.6 Even though it has been said that man is affected by good or bad company, but Chanakya believes that a gentleman is not affected by being in evil man's company, for any period of time. Like the sandalwood tree does not become poisonous, even though poisonous snakes rest on it and like the flower which grows in the soil, does not carry its smell, similarly a gentleman who remains in the company of evil persons, does not shed his righteousness and good deeds.

Sādhūnāṃ Darśanaṃ Puṇyaṃ Tīrthabhūtā Hi Sādhava:.
Kālēna Phalatē Tīrthaṃ Sadya: Sādhusamāgama:..

12.7 A meeting with a gentleman or a saint can get you their sacred blessings whereas to get the blessings from the holy shrines, we need to undertake long trips.

Viprāsminnagarē Mahān Kathaya Kastāladrumāṇāṃ Gaṇa:
Kō Dātā Rajakō Dadāti Vasanaṃ Prātargṛhītvā Niśi.
Kō Dakṣa: Paradāravittaharaṇē Sarvōpi Dakṣō Jana:
Kasmājjīvasi Hē Sakhē Viṣakṛminyāyēna Jīvāmyaham..

12.8 A stranger asked a Brahmin, "who is great in this city?" The Brahmin replied "The cluster of palm trees." The stranger asked again, "Who is the most benevolent person?" The Brahmin replied, "Washer man who collects the clothes in the morning and returns them in the evening." He again questioned, "Who is the most able person?" The Brahmin replied, "Everyone is able in stealing other's wives and wealth." The stranger again asked, "How can you live in such a city?" The Brahmin replied, "like a worm lives in filth." In this shloka, Chanakya has highlighted the rampant faults in the society.

Na Viprapādōdakakardamāni Na Vēdaśāstradhvanigarjitāni.
Svāhā-Svadhākāra-Vivarjitāni Śmaśānatulyāni Gṛhāṇi Tāni..

12.9 Chanakya has considered that home like a crematorium, where Brahmins are not respected/honoured, whose residents are averse to donating, where study and reading of Vedas is not practised, where havan/yagna are not performed. He says that such an abode is filled with ignorance, poverty, sickness, sorrows and difficulties. The persons residing in such a home are like corpses. Therefore, for enjoying happy family life, men should continue to perform acts of worship/prayer, donation and Brahmin reverence.

Satyaṃ Mātā Pitā Jñānaṃ Dharmō Bhrātā Dayā Sva Sā.
Śānti: Patnī Kṣamā Putra: Ṣaḍētē Mama Bāndhavā:..

12.10 In this shloka, Chanakya has identified the true companions of a person bereft of allurement/wealth. He says that for a recluse, truth is like a mother, knowledge is like a father, religion is like a brother, compassion is like a sister, peace is like a wife and forgiveness is like a son. In reality, in this destructible world, they are the true relations/friends. That is why, even a recluse is not alone.

Anityāni Śarīrāṇi Vibhavō Naiva Śāśvata:.
Nityaṃ Saninahitō Mṛtyu: Kartavyō Dharmasaṅgraha:..

12.11 Life and death are the two faces of a coin. A man's body starts with life and ends with death. That is why, the body has been called destructible. Beauty, youth, strength, intelligence—everything gets gradually destroyed. Nobody knows when his end will come. So, Chanakya has advised a man to be duty-conscious. He says that every moment man should be involved in performing good deeds. In it lies his welfare.

Āmantraṇōtsavā Viprā Gāvō Navatṛṇōtsavā:.
Patyutsāhayutā Nārya: Ahaṃ Kṛṣṇa-Raṇōtsava:..

12.12 In this shloka, Chanakya describes different type of pleasure providing things for different living species. He says for a Brahmin, an invitation to a feast is very pleasing. For cows, availability of green grass everyday is pleasing. For women, it is pleasing if their husbands are in full spirits everyday. But for himself, Chanakya finds pleasure in conflict. He says that destruction of war is like a celebration for him.

Mātṛvat Paradārāṃśca Paradravyāṇi Lōṣṭhavat.
Ātmavat Sarvabhūtāni Ya: Praśyati Sa Paśyati..

12.13 Chanakya says that the persons who consider others' women as mothers, others' wealth as dirt and treat others as equals, as saintsgentlemen. That is the persons with character, tolerance, contentment, generosity and compassion are the true gentlemen.

Dharmē Tatparatā Mukhē Madhuratā Dānē Samutsāhatā
Mitrēvañcakatā Gurau Vinayatā Cittēti Gambhīratā.
Ācārē Śucitā Guṇē Rasikatā Śāstrēṣu Vijñānatā
Rūpē Sundaratā Śivē Bhajanatā Tvayyasti Bhō Rāghava:..

12.14 A gentleman is bestowed with virtues. He has qualities like feeling for religion, sweet nature, willingness to donate, affability, respect for Gurus, maturity, politeness, generosity, knowledge of scriptures, good taste and pleasant nature. Against this, the persons without these qualities are evil persons.

Kāṣṭhaṃ Kalpataru: Sumēruracalaścintāmaṇi: Prastara:
Sūryastavrakara: Śaśī Kṣayakara: Kṣārō Hi Vārāṃ Nidhi:.
Kāmō Naṣṭatanurbalidritisutō Nityaṃ Paśu: Kāmagau-
Rnaitāṃstē Tulayāmi Bhō Raghupatē Kasyōpamā Dīyatē..

12.15 In this shloka, Chanakya says that God is supreme. He believes that only God is powerful, extremely kind-hearted, ruler of all the three worlds and all-pervading. Explaining this, he says that the 'Kalpavriksha' fulfills all the desires of a man, but it is only wood. The 'Sumeruparvat' has deposits of vast treasurers, but it is only stone. The Sun's rays are illuminating but are intense, whereas the Moon illuminates and cools but is spotted. The sea inspite of being vast contains salty water and 'Kamdeva' is without a body. Even though 'Bali' is considered a great donor, he belongs to the demon race. Similarly, 'Kamdhenu' who fulfills all the desires of man, is a cow. Oh Lord! None of these unlike you are blemishless, radiant, tolerant, generous and devotee loving; no one can compare with you. So, Oh Lord! You are the supreme power.

Vinayaṃ Rājaputrēbhya: Paṇḍitēbhya: Subhāṣitam.
Anṛtaṃ Dyūtakārēbhya: Strībhya: Śikṣēt Kaitavam..

12.16 A man can definitely learn something or the other from the living things around him. Chanakya has established this saying in this shloka. He says that one must imbibe knowledge from wherever he can. Princes have politeness and courtesy. Imbibing these qualities makes man kind hearted. We can learn the art of affectionate-cum-sweet speech from scholars and lying from gamblers. Also we must imbibe the traits of deception/cunning from women.

Anālōkya Vyayaṃ Kartā Hyanātha: Kalahapriya:.
Ātura: Sarvakṣētrēṣu Nara: Śīghraṃ Vinaśyati..

12.17 Spending more than your earning, fighting with others without any reason and mating with all types of women—these three acts propel man and his family towards ruin. So, a man should make all efforts to stay away from these acts, otherwise he will be ruined in no time.

Nāhāraṃ Cintayētprājñō Dharmamēkaṃ Hi Cintayēt.
Āhārō Hi Manuṣyāṇāṃ Janmanā Saha Jāyatē..

12.18 In the present times, some persons are hoarding food items while others are amassing wealth. Addressing such persons, Chanakya says that Oh foolish man! At the time of birth of the child itself, God takes care of his food. Whatever he is destined to get, nobody can snatch it from him. So, instead hoarding food and amassing wealth, focus on being religious. Even animals are able to feed themselves, but only man has the good fortune of earning blessings by performing religious acts. So, perform religious acts and be blessed. This will ensure shaping of your future in this and the other world.

Jalabindunipātēna Kramaśa: Pūryatē Ghaṭa:.
Sa Hētu: Sarvavidyānāṃ Dharmasya Ca Dhanasya Ca..

12.19 In this shloka, Chanakya says that like drops can fill a pot, merging of drops can form a river, by adding pennies, a man can become wealthy. Similarly, by regular study, for man there is no knowledge which is unattainable. Likewise, if a man is involved in religious activities everyday, then he can amass a hoard of blessings. So, a man should spend most of his time in righteous activities.

Vayasa: Pariṇāmēpi Ya: Khala: Khala Ēva Sa:.
Supakvamapi Mādhuryaṃ Nōpayātīndravāruṇam..

12.20 Like a wild pumpkin even after fully ripening does not become sweet that is, it remains bitter, similarly, an evil person, howsoever aged he becomes, retains his cruelty and sins. Even at an elderly age, he continues to scheme. So, a man should be judged on his abilities rather than his age. Only then it is possible to know his true nature.

❑

Chapter 13

Muhūrtaamapi Jīvēta Nara: Śuklēna Karmaṇā.
Na Kalpamapi Kaṣṭēna Lōkadvayavirōdhinā..

13.1 Chanakya considers having a short life-span of doing good deeds better than a purposeless long life-span. He says that a long life with sorrows and sins is very painful. Such a life has no meaning. Against this, if a man's life is filled with good deeds, even a short life is a pleasure. Whatever his age, a man should do good deeds. His welfare rests in it.

Gatē Śōkō Na Kartavyō Bhaviṣyaṃ Naiva Cintayēt.
Vartamānēna Kālēna Pravartantē Vicakṣaṇā:..

13.2 In this shloka, Chanakya, advising persons who reminisce the past and repeatedly feel sorrow or disappointment, says that the past never returns, the events which have happened cannot be changed. So, remembering them repeatedly does not help. Similarly, a man is totally ignorant of what is going to happen in the future. So, worrying about it is also a waste. A man should only focus on the present. If he improves his present, then his future will also be bright.

Svabhāvēna Hi Tuṣyanti Dēvā: Satpuruṣā: Pitā.
Jñātaya: Svannapānābhyāṃ Vākyadānēna Paṇḍitā:..

13.3 Highlighting the importance of good behaviour and nature, Chanakya says that without too much effort, only by good conduct and disposition a man can satisfy a scholar, a gentleman and father. Similarly, by sweet talk, he can please and satisfy friends, relations and Pundits. In other words, for a person with good behaviour and sweet talk, nothing is impossible.

Ahō Bata Vicitrāṇi Caritāni Mahātmanām.
Lakṣmīṃ Tṛṇāya Manyantē Tadbhārēṇa Namanti Ca..

13.4 In this shloka, Chanakya has explained the nature of a gentleman. He says that a saint or gentleman have a strange nature. Whereas most persons commit numerous sinful acts to attain wealth, wealth for them is like a blade of grass or straw. Wealth has no value in their eyes. Even if they become extremely wealthy, they do not display any arrogance or commit any sins. There is no change in their humbleness. Physical pleasure or change in status does not affect their behaviour.

Yasya Snēhō Bhayaṃ Tasya Snēhō Du:Khasya Bhājanam.
Snēhamūlāni Du:Khāni Tāni Tyaktvā Vasēt Sukham..

13.5 Chanakya considers affection to be the root cause of all sorrows. Clarifying this idea in this shloka, Chanakya says that when a man develops affection for someone, then his life is guided by that person. When that person is unhappy, then the person in affection is also unhappy. Similarly, he feels happiness and fear according to that person. Only affection repeatedly pushes his soul towards the life/death cycle. Against this for a man free from affection, all are equal. He is not affected by anyone's sorrow or happiness. He maintains the same feelings for everyone in his heart. So, a scholar should shed excessive affection and lead a happy life.

Anāgatavidhātā Ca Pratyutpannamatistathā.
Dvāvētau Sukhamēdhētē Yadbhaviṣyō Vinaśyati..

13.6 People, who only rely on fate, waste their valuable life. But the persons, who avert crisis by their efforts and continue to confront adverse circumstances, lead a happy life. Chanakya believes that though fate cannot be changed, a man has to live whatever is fated; yet by efforts and actions the fated adverse circumstances can be turned favourable. So, a man should not shy away from efforts.

Rājñidharmiṇi Dharmiṣṭhā: Pāpē Pāpā: Samē Samā:.
Rājānamanuvartantē Yathā Rājā Tathā Prajā:..

13.7 If the king of a kingdom is religious and talented, then the subjects of that kingdom will also be religious and talented. If the king is a sinner, then his subjects will also behave accordingly; because the subjects follow the king. That is why it is said "As the king, so are his subjects".

Jīvantaṃ Mṛtavanmanyē Dēhinaṃ Dharmavarjitam.
Mṛtō Dharmēṇa Saṃyuktō Dīrghajīvī Na Saṃśaya:..

13.8 Since a criminal always promotes sin, immorality and wrong acts, he only damages the society. According to Chanakya, a criminal may be alive, but is like a dead person. Against this, a person, who has performed auspicious and good deeds, is remembered even after his death. His reputation and fame keep him alive. So, a man should try to earn respect/honour and fame by his good deeds, so that even after his death, his memory lives.

Dharmārthakāmamōkṣāṇāṃ Yasyaikōpi Na Vidyatē.
Ajāgalastanasyēva Tasya Janma Nirarthakam..

13.9 Religious scriptures list four valours—religion, economics, sex and salvation. Of these, economics and sex have been called the valours of this world and religion and salvation have been called the valours for the other world. All four provide purpose to human life. Without these valours, the life is a waste. So, a man should try to achieve at least one valour.

Dahyamānā: Sutīvrēṇa Nīcā: Para Yaśōgninā.
Aśaktastatpadaṃ Gantuṃ Tatō Nindāṃ Prakurvatē..

13.10 Describing the thought process and behaviour of cruel and evil persons, Chanakya says that it is the fundamental nature of evil persons to envy the progress of others. Apart from trying to advance themselves, they try to put down others. But on failing, they resort to criticising to uplift themselves and degrade others. This is how they try to prove an able person, to be inept. A person having such thoughts is an evil person.

Bandhāya Viṣayāsaktaṃ Muktyai Nirviṣayaṃ Mana:.
Mana Ēva Manuṣyāṇāṃ Kāraṇaṃ Bandhamōkṣayō:..

13.11 In this shloka, Chanakya believes that the mind is the root cause of all bonds and sorrows. He says that God provides the soul, human life, only for its salvation. But a man gets attracted towards weaknesses like sex, anger, greed, liquor, affection, etc. and goes astray from his aim. The sole reason for this is the mind.

It is only the mind which pushes a man towards the sense of sexual enjoyment and leads him towards sins. A man under the hypnosis of the mind can never free himself from the cycle of life death. So, a man should contain all weaknesses of the mind and exercise control over it. Only then it will be possible for him to improve his life in the other world.

Dēhābhimānē agalitē Vijñātē Paramātmani.
Yatra Yatra Manō Yātitatratatra Samādhaya:..

13.12 Human body is destructible, so, a man should not be conceited about it. Any man, who sheds conceit and develops the passion for worshipping God in his mind, then wherever his mind wanders, he still can meditate. Anyone, who is able to understand the true relationship between body and soul, can meditate irrespective of the circumstances.

Īpsitaṃ Manasa: Sarvaṃ Kasya Sampadyatē Sukham.
Dēvāyattaṃ Yata: Sarvaṃ Tasmāt Santōṣamāśrayēt..

13.13 One should give up the desire for all kinds of wishes and pleasures. Everything is in Gods hands—he decides who gets what and who gives what. So, everyone should learn to be satisfied with what they have.

Karmāyattaṃ Phalaṃ Puṃsāṃ abuddhi: Karmānusāriṇī.
Tathāpi Sudhayaśçāryā: Suviçāryaiva Kurvatē..

13.14 A man desires numerous wishes; some are fulfilled and others are not. The fulfilment of the wishes depends on fate and his actions. His fate decides the rewards based on his actions. If a man wishes for worldly pleasures in return for·his bad deeds, then his wish will never be fulfilled. So, man should perform good deeds for favourable rewards.

Yathā Dhēnusahasrēṣu Vatsō Gacchati Mātaram.
Tathā Yacca Kṛtaṃ Karma Kartāramanugacchati..

13.15 It is the law of nature that you shall reap what you sow. Like the calf can identify its mother amongst hundreds of cows, the act identifies its originator. In fact, a man's actions and its results are linked. So, perform only good deeds to expect favourable rewards.

Anavasthitakāryasya Na Janē Na Vanē Sukham.
Janē Dahati Saṃsargō Vanē Saṅgavivarjanam..

13.16 Persons, who lead aimless life, can neither find peace at home nor in the forest. Their life is like a dead weight which benefits no one. So, to have an aim in life is essential. Persons who decide on their life's aim never go astray.

Yathā Khātvā Khanitrēṇa Bhūtalē Vāri Vindati.
Tathā Gurugatāṃ Vidyāṃ Śuśrūṣuradhigacchati..

13.17 In this shloka, Chanakya clarifies the importance of dedication. He says that any task undertaken with full dedication never fails to reward. Like a labourer toils and digs the earth with a spade, is able to extract underground water, similarly, a student should learn the knowledge stored with his Guru by dedicated service.

Ēkākṣarapradātāraṃ Yō Guruṃ Nābhivandati.
Śvānayōniśataṃ Bhuktvā Cāṇḍālēṣvabhijāyatē..

13.18 In the 'Vedas' and 'Puranas', the single letter 'Om' has been called the creation 'Mantra' (hymn). Chanakya has expressed its importance in this shloka. He says that by reciting the 'Om Mantra', a man can easily secure the divine knowledge related with Brahma. The person, who preaches the divine knowledge, gives the right direction to the society. Such a Guru must always be revered. But anyone, who disrespects them, after bearing extreme suffering in the form of a dog, will be born in the form of a demon.

Yugāntē Pracalatē Mēru: Kalpāntē Sapta Sāgarā:.
Sādhava: Pratipannārthān Na Caalanti Kadācana..

13.19 Chanakya agrees that at the end of this age, the 'Sumeru' mountain will be displaced, all the seven seas will cross their limits and submerge the earth. But he believes that even in such a crisis, great men and saints will remain steadfast on their vow and resolve. Such gentlemen are trustworthy. Only because of such persons, this earth is protected from calamities.

❑

Chapter 14

Pṛthivyāṃ Trīṇi Ratnāni Jalamagnaṃ Subhāṣitam.
Mūḍhai: Pāṣāṇakhaṇḍēṣu Ratnasañjñā Vidhīyatē..

14.1 According to Chanakya, diamond, pearl, emerald, gold, etc. are like pieces of stone. He says amongst all the jewels on earth—water, food and sweet talk are the most precious jewels. Water and food help a man to survive; nourish his body and enhance his strength/wisdom. By sweet talk even the enemy can be befriended. But if any person hankers after the stones, leaving these jewels, his entire life is filled with sorrows. Even though one can live without those stones, it is hard to imagine survival without these valuable jewels.

Ātmāparādhavṛkṣasya Phalānyētāni Dēhinām.
Dāridryarōgadu:Khāni Bandhanavyasanāni Ca..

14.2 A man is rewarded or punished according to his deeds. Nobody can change this law of nature. The sorrows, griefs, worries, restrictions and crises which, a man faces in his life, are the consequences of his sinful deeds. Against this his good deeds will enable him to live a sorrow- and conflict-free happy life. So, a man should perform superior deeds.

Punarvittaṃ Punarmitraṃ Punarbhāryā Punarmahī.
Ētatsarvaṃ Punarlabhayaṃ Na Śarīraṃ Puna: Puna:..

14.3 Even though wealth, property, friends, woman and kingdom can be obtained repeatedly, human form is attained only once. Once it is annihilated, it is impossible to attain it again. So, a man should perform good deeds and use it for worthy causes. Only the life of people, who perform good deeds everyday, is a success.

Bahūnāṃ Caiva Sattvānāṃ Samavāyō Ripuñjaya:.
Varṣadharādharō Mēghastṛṇairapi Nivāryatē..

14.4 "There is great strength in unity" this saying is famous from times immemorial. Chanakya has explained this saying in this shloka. He says that like a group of hyenas can fight a lion, a roof made of bundle of straws stops water, similarly, if many weak persons unite, then they can face even the mightiest person.

Jalē Tailaṃ Khalē Guhyaṃ Pātrē Dānaṃ Manāgapi.
Prājñē Śāstraṃ Svayaṃ Yāti Vistāraṃ Vastuśakitata:..

14.5 In this shloka, Chanakya says that if a drop of oil is dropped in a bowl of water, it spreads all over. An evil person cannot keep a secret; he spreads it in no time. Even if an intelligent person gains a little knowledge, he is able to learn more. Similarly, Chanakya says that if donation is given to a deserving person, then it is received back by the donor ten-fold.

Dharmākhyānē Śmaśānē Ca Rōgiṇāṃ Yā Matirbhavēt.
Sā Sarvadaiva Tiṣṭhēccēt Kō Na Mucyēta Bandhanāt..

14.6 In this shloka, Chanakya has told about a man's restless nature. He says that a man's nature lacks stability, so it keeps changing every minute. He develops the feelings of a recluse when he listens to a religious discourse or when he sees a corpse in a crematorium, the worldly attachment/wealth seems worthless to him. But after his return from there, he again gets trapped in the material world and starts amassing. This restlessness is the biggest stumbling block, in his attaining salvation. So, a man should adopt all the possible means to control it.

Utpannapaścāttāpasya Buddhirbhavati Yādṛśī.
Tādṛśī Yadi Pūrva Syāt Kasya Na Syānmahōdaya:..

14.7 It is usually seen that a man's conscious is stirred after performing bad or derogatory deeds and the feeling of regret sets in. But if realises what is good or bad before indulging in bad deeds, then he will be get rid of doing the bad deeds forever. An evil person into the mire of bad deeds disgraces not only himself but his family also. So, one must refrain from doing derogatory deeds.

Dānē Tapasi Śauryē Vā Vijñānē Vinayē Nayē.
Vismayō Na Hi Kartavyō Bahuratnā Vasundharā..

14.8 Whenever a man achieves supremacy or success in any work, he develops a sense of arrogance. Cautioning on this state, Chanakya says that the world is full of exceptional donors, devotees, gallant, worshippers and intelligent people. So, a man should not become arrogant, on his ability of donation, devotion, bravery, worship, courage, knowledge of science, politeness and strategic prowess.

Anyone, who becomes arrogant, sins in a hurry and is ruined.

Dūrasthōpi Na Dūrasthō Yō Yasya Manasi Sthita:.
Yō Yasya Hṛdayē Nāsti Samīpasthōpi Dūrata:..

14.9 In this shloka, Chanakya tells about the significance of true love. He says that the bond of true love binds mutually to great depths. In such a state, even if one is away, the other feels him to be close by. In contrast, if there is no affection, then even if the other person is close by, there is detachment. Expanding on this argument, Chanakya says that if a man develops affectionate attachment with God, then he is always close by. So, man should tie affectionate bonding with God by worship.

Yasya Cāpriyamicchēta Tasya Brūyāt Sadā Priyam.
Vyādhō Mṛgavadhaṃ Kartuṃ Gītaṃ Gāyati Susvaram..

14.10 On the benefits of sweet talk, Chanakya says that like the snake charmer charms the snake with his flute, the hunter tames the deer, similarly, a man can control anyone by sweet talk. He can win over enemies by sweet talk and all his wishes are fulfilled.

Atyāsannā Vināśāya Dūrasthā Na Phalapradā:.
Sēvitavyaṃ Madhyabhāgēna Rājā Vahnirguru: Striya:..

14.11 King, fire, Guru and woman, according to Chanakya, for all the four, neither their proximity nor their avoidance is good; it can lead to a man's complete ruin. The proximity to king and Guru makes him arrogant and becomes blemished; whereas staying away leads to neglect. The nearness to fire results in burning and turning to ash; whereas staying away from it diminishes its heat and light. Closeness to woman generates many flaws, whereas separation might cause her to go astray. To safeguard from this situation, Chanakya says that a man should find a solution by taking a middle path. He should remain neither too close nor too far from them.

aagnirāpa: Striyō Mūrkhā: Sarpā Rājakulāni Ca.
Nityaṃ Yatnēna Sēvyāni Sadya: Prāṇaharāṇi Ṣaṭ..

14.12 In this shloka, Chanakya has described certain things/people where man needs to exercise caution while dealing with them. He says that fire, water, woman, fool, snake and royal family while they are useful for a man, but may be ruinous for him if he is careless. So, they must be dealt with due caution.

Sa Jīvati Guṇā Yasya Yasya Dharma: Sa Jīvati.
Guṇadharmavihīnasya Jīvitaṃ Niṣprayōjanam..

14.13 Chanakya considers the life of such persons meaningful who have the qualities of compassion, love, welfare, tolerance, etc. In fact, according to him, only such persons deserve to live life. Life is meaningless, if these qualities are missing. Therefore, a man should imbibe these qualities, so that his life is successful.

Yadīcchasī Vaśīkartuṃ Jagadēkēna Karmaṇā.
Parāpavādasasyēbhyō Gāṃ Carantīṃ Nivāraya..

14.14 In this shloka, Chanakya, clarifying his opinion on criticising others, says that it is the most depraving and dreadful deed. If a man can give it up, then he can control the entire world. In other words, by giving up criticising, all the pleasures will favour a man.

Prastāvasadṛśaṃ Vākyaṃ Prabhāvasadṛśaṃ Priyam.
Ātmaśakitasamaṃ Kōpaṃ Yō Jānāti Sa Paṇḍita:..

14.15 According to Chanakya, only that person is intelligent, who speaks at the right time, who shows heroism according to his strength and displays anger as per his capacity. If however, a man digresses from the topic of discussion does not consider his strength and gets angry unnecessarily, then he is considered an intelligent fool.

Ēka Ēva Padārthastu Tridhā Bhavati Vīkṣita:.
Kuṇapa: Kāminī Māṃsaṃ Yōgibhi: Kāmibhi: Śvabhi:..

14.16 In this shloka, Chanakya says that different people have different perspective for a particular thing. For a saint, a woman is like a corpse, but to a lusty person, she appears like an image of looks/beauty. For a hyena, she is nothing but a lump of meat. Here Chanakya clarifies that it is the man's point of view which enhances or depreciates the value of a thing. It appears as if he wishes to see it.

Susiddhamōṣadhaṃ Dharmaṃ Gṛhacchidraṃ Ca Maithunam.
Kubhuktaṃ Kuśrutaṃ Caiva Matimānna Prakāśayēt..

14.17 Chanakya has advised scholars to keep certain things secret. He says that a scholar should never discuss with others his knowledge of an unfailing medicine, his religious customs, his domestic problems, about his sex with a woman, bad food and abusive discussions. One should keep such things to oneself. If he discusses such things with others, then his being a scholar is useless. He will be compared to a fool.

Tāvanmaunēna Nīyantē Kōkilaiścaiva Vāsarā:.
Yāvatsarvajanā Nandadāyinī Vākpravartatē..

14.18 Till spring arrives, the cuckoo remains quiet, but once spring arrives, Cuckoo spreads his melodious voice in all the directions. By quoting this example, Chanakya has given a very meaningful advice to scholars. He says that only at the right time intelligent people should take up the tasks suited for that time. Against this, people who undertake tasks unmindful of the time always fail.

Dharmaṃ Dhanaṃ Ca Dhānyaṃ Ca Gurōrvacanamauṣadham.
Sugṛhītaṃ Ca Kartavyamanyathā Tu Na Jīvati..

14.19 If there is a slip in religious activities, then it does not yield any reward. If life-saving medicines are not used as directed, they can be life threatening. Excessive waste of food and wealth leads to poverty. You will face several hardships by not following Guru's orders properly. Therefore, Chanakya has directed that religion, medicines, wealth, paddy and Guru's orders must be carefully handled.

Tyaja Durjanasaṃsargaṃ Bhaja Sādhusamāgamam.
Kuru Puṇyamahōrātraṃ Smara Nityamanityātām..

14.20 People, who have a strong concern for self-welfare, guiding them, Chanakya says that they should shun the company of evil persons and join the company of gentlemen. Its effect will destroy sexual lust, as well as, impure thoughts and a man will move towards the right path. That is by giving up affection wealth and sexual lust, a man should get engrossed in God worship and charity. His well-being lies in it.

❑

Chapter 15

Yasya Cittaṃ Dravībhūtaṃ Kṛpayā Sarvajantuṣu.
Tasya Jñānēna Mōkṣēṇa Kiṃ Jaṭābhasmalēpanai:..

15.1 Stating that amongst all the good deeds, kindness is the most superior, Chanakya says that anyone, whose heart is filled with happiness, by being kind to others, does not require to grow matted hair (*jataaye*) or apply ash (*bhasma*) to gain knowledge and salvation. Even after hundreds of years of self-mortification (*tapasya*) what is even rare for ascetics, that knowledge and salvation can be obtained easily by being kind to mankind. By imbibing this quality, a man finds a place in the list of dignitaries. So, the feeling of kindness must always be preserved in the heart.

Ēkamēvākṣaraṃ Yastu Guru: Śiṣyaṃ Prabōdhayat.
Pṛthivyāṃ Nāsti Taddravyaṃ Yaddatvā Cānṛṇī Bhavēt..

15.2 From the Vedic times, Gurus have been called the source of gaining knowledge. Chanakya has also described the greatness of Gurus in this shloka. He says that a man learns the deep secrets of Brahma-Shakti, Soul-God and knowledge of the elements from the Guru only. With the blessings of the Guru only, a man breaks free from the arena of affection/wealth and becomes capable to come face-to-face with Brahma. In fact, the Guru acts like a bridge between God and worshipper. The debts of such a Guru cannot be repaid even by the most valuable things on earth.

Khalānāṃ Kaṇṭakānāṃ Ca Dvividhaiva Pratikriyā.
Upānānmukhabhaṅgōṃ Vā Dūratō Vā Visarjanam..

15.3 In this shloka, Chanakya has advised gentlemen to stay away from evil persons. Suggesting the solution, Chanakya says they are like thorns, so either crush them with your shoes or take an alternate path. That is either finish them or stay away from them.

Kucailinaṃ Dantamalōpasṛṣṭaṃ Bahmavāśinaṃ Niṣṭhurabhāṣiṇaṃ Ca.
Sūryōdayē Cāstamitē Śayānaṃ Vimuñcati Śrīryadi Cakrapāṇi:..

15.4 Through this shloka, Chanakya has described about physical cleanliness, habits and religious practices. According to him, those who wear dirty clothes, whose teeth are dirty, who overeat, who use offensive language, and who sleep during sunrise or sunset, such persons lose their grace, health, beauty and even God deserts them. Everyone avoids such persons, howsoever rich they may be or even if they belong to the highest caste.

Tyajanti Mitrāṇi Dhanairvihīnaṃ Dārāśca Bhṛtyāśca Suhṛjjanāśca.
Taṃ Cārthavantaṃ Punarāśrayantē Arthō Hi Lōkē Puruṣasya Bandhu:..

15.5 Explaining the wonders of wealth, Chanakya says that if a man becomes rich, then even strangers become familiar; wife, son, friends, relations also express affection and become personal. But if some rich person turns poor, even near the ones distance themselves. Wife, son, friends, near ones, relations leave him one after another. This shows that wealth is a true well-wisher of a man. Anyone, who has wealth, also controls happiness.

Anyāyōpārjitaṃ Dravyaṃ Daśa Varṣāṇi Tiṣṭhati.
Prāptē Caikādaśē Varṣē Samūlaṃ Tadra Vinaśyati..

15.6 For getting wealth, a man commits many derogatory acts. But Chanakya says that wealth earned like that is dissipative. He says that wealth earned by sinning and malpractice lasts at the most for ten years. In the eleventh year, he loses all this wealth with interest. Against this, wealth earned through hard work and honesty is retained lifelong and it keeps growing. So, a man should refrain from earning wealth by sinning.

Ayuktaṃ Svāminō Yuktaṃ Yuktaṃ Nīcasya Dūṣaṇam.
Amṛtaṃ Rāhavē Mṛtyurviṣaṃ Śaṅkarabhūṣaṇam..

15.7 A man's influence in the society is very important. For 'Rahu' (mythological dragons head), even nectar killed him, whereas for Lord Shiva, even the poison consumed by him turned to nectar. Even after consuming poison, he was alive and became famous as 'Neelkanth' (person with blue neck). In other words, even an improper act committed by an influential person seems proper to people. Against this, even a proper act performed by an inadequate person draws suspicion of the people. Doubts are expressed over it.

**Tad Bhōjanaṃ Yad Dvijabhuktaśēṣaṃ Tatsauhṛdaṃ Yat Kriyatē Parisman.
Sa Prājñatā Yā Na Karōti Pāpaṃ Dambhaṃ Vinā Ya: Kriyatē Sa Dharma:..**

15.8 Chanakya considers the food left over after feeding the Brahmins till contentment, as superior food. Similarly, the love for others, according to him, is true love. He considers the person, who does not commit sins, to be intelligent; the religion which protects from sins, falsehood and derogatory acts, as the true religion.

**Maṇirluṇṭhati Pādāgrē Kāca: Śirasi Dhāryatē.
Krayavikrayavēlāyāṃ Kāca: Kācō Maṇirmaṇi:..**

15.9 Even if the diamond is tied to the feet and glass is adorned on the head, it does not diminish the value of the diamond. Likewise, placing a scholar on a lower seat and the fool on a higher seat, does not diminish the status of the scholar. The scholar will be compared with scholars and the fool will be counted amongst fools. For a scholar, a higher or lower level has no meaning.

**Anantaśāstraṃ Bahulāśca Vidyā: Alpaśca Kālō Bahuvighnatā Ca.
Yatsārabhūtaṃ Tadupāsanīyaṃ Haṃsō Yathā Kṣīra Mivāmbumadhyāt..**

15.10 Commenting on knowledge, Chanakya says that this world is filled with immense knowledge. The human soul, even after taking hundreds of births, cannot learn all the knowledge. But like the swan can drink only the milk from diluted milk and leave the water, similarly, a man like the swan should extract the essential elements like milk from the many scriptures and other studies. That is, a man should fully understand the meaning of the Vedas in the short span of his life.

Dūrāgataṃ Pathi Śrāntaṃ Vṛthā Ca Gṛhamāgatam.
Anarcayitvā Yō Bhuṅktē Sa Vai Cāṇḍāla Ucyatē..

15.11 The guests who come from distant places, tired travelers and people seeking shelter are like God. So, a man should first feed them their fill and then eat himself. But the persons, who eat themselves first without feeding them are like demons.

Paṭhanti Caturō Vēdān Dharmaśāstrāṇyanēkaśa:.
Ātmānaṃ Naiva Jānanti Darvī Pākarasaṃ Yathā..

15.12 People, who even after studying religious scriptures like Vedas, etc. remain ignorant of its essential elements, who do not have knowledge of Soul-God, remain devoid of knowledge of their own spiritual self. Chanakya has compared such persons with a ladle, which stirs the juicy curry but which remains unaware of its taste and usefulness. Chanakya says that such a study is a waste.

Dhanyā Dvijamayī Naukā Viparītā Bhavārṇavē.
Tarantyadhōgatā: Sarvē Uparisthā: Patantyadha:..

15.13 In this shloka, highlighting the importance of Brahmins, Chanakya says that Brahmin in the *avatar* of a boat, always moves in the opposite direction in the world in the *avatar* of the sea. People, who take shelter under the deck of the boat, cross the sea, whereas the people on the deck of the boat drown in the sea. That is, the world of allurement wealth pushes one towards sexual lusts. In this world, Brahmin is the only boat which moves in the opposite direction and heads towards salvation. Persons, who consider Brahmins above all, are in their service, who pay obeisance to their feet and behave as they do, attain salvation.

Against this, persons who consider themselves superior to Brahmins, who insult them, are unable to free themselves from the life-death cycle. They are reborn again and again, from different 'Yonis' (organ of generation) and bear untold sufferings.

Ayamamṛtanidhānaṃ Nāyakōpyauṣadhīnāṃ
Amṛtamayaśarīra: Kāntiyuktōapi Candra:.
Bhavati Vigataraśmirmaṇḍalaṃ Prāpya Bhānō:
Parasadananiviṣṭa Kō Laghutvaṃ Na Yāti..

15.14 Even though the Moon is said to be the storehouse of nectar, lord of medicines, immortal and lustrous, once the Sun rises over the horizon, all its radiance is lost and it becomes lusterless and disappears. Similarly, if a person goes to anyone's house as a beggar, then his respect, honour and pride are ruined. Therefore, a man should labour, so that the need to beg does not arise.

Alirayaṃ Nalinīdalamadhyaga: Kamalinīmakarandamadālasa:.
Vidhivaśāt Paradēśamupāgata: Kuṭajapuṣparasaṃ Bahu Manyatē..

15.15 Chanakya says that in a foreign place, a man should mould himself according to the situation and his income. Like the beetle that normally lives in the lily leaves and is used to being immersed in the juice from its pollen but in a foreign place, it has to be satisfied with the odourless and tasteless juice of the thorny bush. Likewise in a foreign place a man should be satisfied with the available food. It will facilitate him to change favourably for that place.

Pīta: Kruddhēna Tātaścaraṇatalahatō Vallabhō Yēna Rōṣād
Ābālyād Vipravaryai: Svavadanavivarē Dhāryatē Vairiṇī Mē.

Gēhaṃ Sē Chēdayanti Pratidivasamumākāntapūjānimittaṃ
Tasmāt Khinnā Sadāhaṃ Dvijakulanilayaṃ Nātha Yuktaṃ Tyajāmi..

15.16 In this shloka, Chanakya has presented a dialogue between Lord Vishnu and Goddess Lakshmi. Once Lord Vishnu asked Goddess Lakshmi "Why are you displeased with the Brahmins"? Then Goddess Lakshmi replied "Oh Lord! Hermit Agastya in his anger had gulped my father, the Ocean. The great Saint Brighu had kicked you in the chest. The superior Brahmins worship my sister Goddess Saraswati, instead of me. They keep on uprooting lotus flowers from my abode to pray/worship Lord Shiva. That is why, I am displeased with the Brahmins".

Even though this dialogue appears to be ordinary, through it, Chanakya has shown that Brahmins never give importance to wealth. For them, there is nothing more important than God's worship.

Bandhaanāni Khalu Santi Bahūni Prēmarajjudṛdhabandhanamanyat.
Dārubhēdanipuṇōpi Ṣaḍaṅghirniṣkriyō Bhaavati Paṅkajakōśē..

15.17 Chanakya has called the love-bond to be most superior to all other bonds. In this context, he says that the beetle that has the capability to bore wood, becomes inert when closeted inside the delicate lotus flower. That is because he loves the lotus flower and the fear of causing any damage to it, makes him inert. He loves the beauty of the lotus. He fears that as soon as its beauty ends, its love will also end. So, he ends his life for the sake of its love.

Chinnōpi Candanatarurna Jahāti Gandhaṃ
Vṛddhōpi Vāraṇapatirna Jahāti Līlām.

Yantrārpitō Madhuratāṃ Na Jahāti Cēkṣu:
Kṣīṇōpi Na Tyajati Śīlaguṇān Kulīna:..

15.18 With a man's birth, certain natural qualities manifest themselves and they remain till death. In this context, Chanakya says that even after the sandalwood tree is cut, its fragrance does not disappear, even after the elephant ages, its sexual craving does not cool off, even after the sugarcane is crushed its sweetness does not finish, similarly, when a man born in a high-status family with virtuous qualities becomes poor, his politeness, humility and morality do not disappear. He behaves gracefully even in crisis.

❑

Chapter 16

Na Dhyātaṃ Padamīśvarasya Vidhivatsaṃsāravicchittayē
Svargadvārakapāṭapāṭanapaṭurdharmōpi Nōpārjita:.
Nārīpīnapayōdharōruyugalaṃ Svapnēpi Nāliṅgitaṃ.
Mātu: Kēvalamēva Yauvanavanacchēdē Kuṭhārā Vayam..

16.1 In the Vedas, etc. and other religious scriptures, it has been said that getting a human life form is very singular. It is only after undergoing hardships of several births the soul is fortunate to be born in the human life form. So, instead of wasting the life in sexual lusts, it should be used for attaining salvation. Salvation can only be attained by a man when he sets right his life in this and the other world. In this shloka, Chanakya tells about it. He says that to set right this life, anyone who has not earned sufficient funds, who does not worship God for freeing himself from this worldly illusion, who has never copulated, such a person does not benefit in this world or set right his other world. Such persons only cut the tree in the form of mother's youth with an axe. In other words, their life neither provides any happiness to the mother nor earns them any meaningful credit. So, Chanakya says that a man should enjoy all the worldly pleasures in this world; but at the same time, undertake religious activities to try and improve life in the other world.

Jalpanti Sārdhamanyēna Paśyantyanyaṃ Savibhramā:.
Hṛdayē Cintayantyanyaṃ Na Strīṇāmēkatō Rati:..

16.2 In this shloka, Chanakya has described the playful tendency of women. He says that they have a restless nature. They talk to someone but look lustfully at someone else. They worry about someone in the mind and yearn for someone else in the heart. A woman's love is not for one only. So their affection should not be taken as attachment.

Yō Mōhānmanyatē Mūḍhō Raktēyaṃ Mavi Kāminī.
Sa Tasya Vaśagā Bhūtvā Nṛtyēt Krīḍā-Śakuntavat..

16.3 Any man who thinks that the beautiful woman who shows affection and acts playfully towards him, is in love with him, soon loses everything. He behaves like a puppet and dances on the tune of that woman.

Kōrthān Prāpya Na Garvitō Viṣayiṇa: Kasyāpadōstaṃ Gatā:
Strībhi: Kasya Na Khaṇḍitaṃ Bhuvi Mana: Kō Nāma Rājñāṃ Priya:.
Ka: Kālasya Na Gōcaratvamagamat Kōrthī Gatō Gauravaṃ
Kō Vā Durjanavāgurāsu Patita: Kṣēmēṇa Yāta: Pathi..

16.4 Even though Chanakya was fully aware of the ills of wealth, he had also accepted its importance and influence. He says that the intoxication of wealth is so powerful that on attaining it even a wise/sensible and learned person turns arrogant. The greed for it places a man into difficulties again and again. Intoxicated by it, he gets associated with beautiful women. Thereafter he says that, till today, no man has won over death. Nor has anyone earned respect by being a beggar. There is no one in this world, who has not got into difficulties on account of evil persons. So, it is much better to be rich than be poor.

Na Nirmita: Kēna Na Dr̥ṣṭapūrva: Na Śrūyatē Hēmamaya: Kuraṅga.
Tathāpi Tr̥ṣṇā Raghunandanasya Vināśakālē Viparītabuddhi..

16.5 In adverse times, a man loses his wisdom and sense. Even scholars in the midst of a crisis lose their ability to think and understand. In this context, citing an example, Chanakya says that a person in the midst of a crisis loses his sense, like Lord Rama did when he chased a golden deer. Even though he knew that there are no golden deers, he chased it to capture it. That is to say that in adverse times, even intelligent persons act foolish.

Guṇairuttamatāṃ Yāti Nōccairāsanasaṃsthita:.
Prāsādaśikharasthōpi Kāka: Kiṃ Garuḍāyatē..

16.6 In this shloka, Chanakya has accepted the importance of eminent qualities and virtuosity. He says that on account of them, even an ordinary person advances towards the top. Like a crow sitting on top of a building does not become an eagle, similarly, a person occupying a high seat does not become great. For greatness, a man must possess good qualities and be virtuous. By having them, even if he is born in a lower caste, he can get respect/honour in the society.

Guṇā: Sarvatra Pūjyantē Na Mahatyōpi Sampada:.
Pūrṇēndu Kiṃ Tathā Vandyō Niṣkalaṅkō Yatā Kr̥śa:..

16.7 Between having wealth and possessing eminent qualities, Chanakya has said that the latter is more influential and important. He says that in the society, good qualities are respected. So, having lots of wealth has no meaning. Like instead of the full Moon, the smaller Moon of the next day is worshipped, similarly, a poor person of lower caste possessing good qualities is treated respectfully.

Para-Prōktaguṇō Yastu Nirguṇōapi Guṇī Bhavēt.
Indrōpi Laghutāṃ Yāti Svayaṃ Prakhyāpitairguṇai:..

16.8 According to Chanakya, a person devoid of virtues, who is praised behind his back, is talented. He says that he earns a respectful place amongst people on account of his talent. Against this, even if the self-praiser is Lord Indra, he cannot get that respect just by having his stature. That is the person, who is praised by the world, truly deserves the respect.

Vivēkinamanuprāptā Guṇā Yānti Manōjñatām.
Sutarāṃ Ratnamābhāti Cāmīkaraniyōjitam..

16.9 Like a jewel becomes more attractive when it is laid in gold, whereas if it laid in iron, it loses its grace, similarly, if a wise person is talented, then it is most appropriate. By his wisdom, making proper use of his talent, he takes care of the welfare of not only the society, but also of his family. So, it is necessary for a talented person to be wise.

Guṇai: Sarvajñatulyōpi asīdatyēkō Nirāśraya:.
Anarghyamapi Māṇikyaṃ Hēmāśrayamapēkṣatē..

16.10 Until such time a talented and wise person does not get his rightful place, he remains worthless and humiliated. The situation is like that of the diamond still under the ground, which not having reached its rightful place, is treated like a stone. Only when it is laid in gold, then the viewers praise it. Likewise only when a talented person gets to his rightful place, his talents are accepted by the society.

Atiklēśēna Ya Cārthā Dharmasyātikramēṇa Tu.
Śatrūṇāṃ Praṇipātēna Tē Hyarthā Mā Bhavantu Mē..

16.11 Wealth obtained by sinful acts or by causing suffering/ distress to someone, becomes cursed and ruins a man. Such wealth causes even gentlemen to take the path of sin. One must avoid such wealth otherwise very soon he will be ruined along with his family.

Kiṃ Tayā Kriyatē Lakṣmyā Yā Vadhūriva Kēvalā.
Cā Tu Vēśyēva Sā Mānyā Pathikaiarapi Bhujyatē..

16.12 According to Chanakya, wealth is important and useful, only if it does not belong to one person but benefits the whole society. In this context, he says that the wealth amassed for the use of one person is like the virtuous woman of a noble family, who gives pleasure to him only. So her being or not being does not make any difference to the society. Against this the wealth, which is like a prostitute who satisfies and gives pleasure to all the residents apart from the visitors, is useful. So, instead of amassing wealth for vested interests, it should be used for the welfare of the society.

Dhanēṣu Jīvitavyēṣu Strīṣu Cāhārakarmasu.
Atṛptā: Prāṇina: Sarvē Yātā Yāsyanti Yānti Ca..

16.13 In this shloka, Chanakya has clarified that a man is never contented with wealth, life, woman and food items. As much as he gets them, they still remain insufficient. A man is born with dissatisfaction/discontent and leaves this world with them. There is no end to his desire. He always remains agitated and distressed. So, a man should try to save himself from it.

Kṣīyantē Sarvadāanāni Yajñahōmabalikriyā:.
Na Kṣīyatē Pātradānamabhayaṃ Sarvadēhinām..

16.14 The Vedas and other religious scriptures describe in detail the importance of not only food, water, clothes and land donation but also of Brahmayagya, Devayagya, etc. and several other holy yagyas. But he says that their relevance is limited till the fulfilment of the fruits of the acts. Once, a man obtains the fruits of the acts, their effect is exhausted. Against this, the donation given to a worthy person is never in vain. Its effect remains even after the fulfilment of the fruits of the act. So, donation should only be given to a worthy person.

Tṛṇaṃ Laghu Tṛṇāttūlaṃ Tūlādapi Ca Yācaka:.
Vāyunā Kiṃ Na Nītōsau Māmayaṃ Yācayiṣyati..

16.15 Everyone is scared of a beggar; near-dear ones, friends, etc. also desert him. They shun helping the needy. This saying has been very eloquently presented by Chanakya in this shloka. He says that a blade of straw and cotton are the lightest things in this world. But the beggar is figuratively even lighter than these two. Even though a slight breeze blows away the blade of grass and cotton, a gale cannot blow away the beggar. Explaining the reasoning behind it, Chanakya says that lest the beggar should demand anything, even the breeze changes its direction, that is, the beggar is humiliated by everyone.

Varaṃ Prāṇaparityāgō Mānabhaṅgēna Jīvanāt.
Prāṇatyāgē Kṣaṇaṃ Du:Khaṃ Mānabhaṅgē Dinē Dinē..

16.16 Chanakya says that being disgraced is more painful and damaging than death. He says that it is appropriate for a disgraced person to die rather than remain alive. A disgraced person is humiliated on every occasion; the society views him with hatred; near-dear ones' and friends' behaviour becomes derogatory towards him. Even his wife and son tend to avoid him. A respectful death gives more relief than living such a life.

Priyavākyapradānēna Sarvē Tuṣyanti Jantava:.
Tasmāttadēva Vaktavyaṃ Vacanē Kā Daridratā..

16.17 Sweet talk delights and pleases the mind. By sweet talk, one can even win over enemies. In this shloka, Chanakya has accepted its importance. He says that a man should always talk sweetly. A melodious voice pleases and delights everyone. Sweet talk does not cost anything. So, give up bitter talk and embrace sweet talk. It is a sure-spell to win over the world.

Saṃsārakaṭuvṛkṣasya Dvē Phalē Amṛtōpamē.
Subhāṣitaṃ Ca Susvādu Saṅgati: Sujanē Janē..

16.18 Considering the world to be a bitter tree, Chanakya says that two sweet and nectar-bearing fruits representing cultured language and company of saints grow on this tree. On the one hand, by using cultured language, it is possible to win over everyone's heart, on the other hand, the company of saints/sages converts even evil persons to gentlemen. So, a man should definitely eat these two fruits.

Janma-Janmanyabhyastaṃ Yad Dānamadhyayanaṃ Tapa:.
Tēnaivābhyāsayōgēna Tadēvābhyasyatē Puna:..

16.19 Good characteristics are carried forward from the previous birth. Being charitable, educated, having restraint, virtue, etc. like good traits are carried forward from several previous births by good fortune in this life also. Life must be made purposeful by making use of them.

Pustakēṣu Ca Yā Vidyā Parahastēṣu Yaddhanam.
Utpannēṣu Ca Kāryēṣu Na Sā Vidyā Na Taddhanam..

16.20 In this shloka, Chanakya has clarified the importance of education and wealth. He says that in the time of need, the knowledge in books and others' wealth does not help. In crisis, only the wealth saved by a man helps. Similarly, the student, who can put the education into practice, can benefit from it in life. So, a man should definitely save wealth for crisis. The students should make good use of the education in life as much as possible.

❑

Chapter 17

Pustakapratyayādhītaṃ Nādhītaṃ Gurusaninadhau.
Sabhāmadhyē Na Śōbhantē Jāragarbhā Iva Striya:..

17.1 To learn any knowledge properly and become proficient in it, a Guru is required. In other words, it is not possible to gain knowledge without a Guru. Chanakya concurs with this ancient saying. He says that a person, who forsakes his Guru, is like that immoral woman, who is humiliated in the society. Even after bearing a son, she remains without the glory associated with motherhood. Any person, who leaves the Gurus *ashram* and wanders around to gain knowledge, even if he gains knowledge from anywhere, he becomes a laughing stock in the gathering of scholars. Such a person, even though he is knowledgeable, is not respected in the society.

Kṛtē Pratikṛtaṃ Kuryād Hiṃsanē Pratihiṃsanam.
Tatra Dōṣō Na Paatati Duṣṭē Duṣṭaṃ Samācarēt..

17.2 'Tit for Tat'—Chanakya supported this saying. He believed there should be a reaction for every action. In other words, a man should retaliate in the same manner as he has been treated. Explaining in detail, Chanakya says that if a man behaves with you like a gentleman, then you must also reciprocate accordingly. However, if a person intends to harm you, then he should also be paid back in the same coin.

Yaddūraṃ Yaddūrārādhyaṃ Yacca Dūrē Vyavasthitam.
Tatsarvaṃ Tapasā Sādhyaṃ Tapō Hi Duratikramam..

17.3 In this shloka, Chanakya has discussed about having devotion for hard work. He says anything which is impossible for a man to achieve, is beyond his limits, can be achieved by devotion or untiring hard work. The power of hard work is limitless; its strength can even make possible the impossible. So, a man should not shy away from hard work; rather he should make all possible efforts and by untiring hard work, make his life happy.

Lōbhaścēdaguṇēna Kiṃ Piśunatā Yadyasti Kiṃ Pātakai:
Satyaṃ Cēttapasā Ca Kiṃ Śuci Manō Yadyasti Tīrthēna Kim.
Saujanyaṃ Yadi Kiṃ Guṇai: Sumahimā Yadyasti Kiṃ Muṇḍanai:
Sadvidyā Yadi Kiṃ Dhanairapayaśō Yadyasti Kiṃ Mṛtyunā..

17.4 In this shloka, Chanakya says that if a man is greedy, then he need not worry about the evil persons, because greed is his biggest enemy, which leads him towards ruin. The criticiser and back-biter need not be concerned by criminals. By criticizing, they themselves act like criminals. No devotion is greater than truth. The blaze of truth eliminates all the perversions of the body. Therefore, there is no need for the truthful person to undertake devotional penance. If a man's mind is polluted and impure, then even by visiting sacred shrines his afflicted heart is not purified. Contrarily, anyone whose heart is clear and pure, there is no need for him to visit sacred shrines. If the heart is filled with affection, then all other qualities are secondary, whereas compared to fame, the radiance of all the jewellery is inferior. After gaining knowledge, a man learns the meaning of life. It becomes easier for him to understand the mystery of Soul-God and sighting of Brahma. Such a person becomes free of the worldly attachments. That is why, he does not need the wealth which leads to sexual lusts. An afflicted person bears suffering and pain every moment and dies. For such a person death is the only way out. So, he should not fear death.

Pitā Ratnākarō Yasya Lakṣmīryasya Sahōdarā.
Śaṅkhō Bhikṣāṭanaṃ Kuryānnādattamupatiṣṭhatē..

17.5 Shankh and Goddess Lakshmi, both are considered to be the children of Ratnakar Ocean. But one of them, Goddess Lakshmi, possesses wealth/affluence and is worshipped in the world, whereas the other wanders around with saints/hermits for alms. Inspite of being the brother of wealthy affluent Goddess Lakshmi, Shankh begs for alms along with the poor and worldly detached hermits. On account of spending his life without donating, after death, he had to become a beggar. That is why, Chanakya says that in order to preserve usefulness of one's knowledge, a man should continue to donate as per his ability. This will ensure his welfare in this and the other world.

Aśaktastu Bhavētsādhurbrahmacārī Ca Nirdhana:.
Vyādhiṣṭhō Dēvabhaktaśca Vṛddhā Nārī Pativratā..

17.6 A man's nature is like the bird flying in the sky. But not having wings makes him helpless and he is forced to walk on the ground. Chanakya considers some helplessness to be beneficial for man. He says that helplessness keeps a man and his character from going astray. The lack of power compels a man to turn celibate; the lack of wealth makes a man to become a saint/hermit and a sick person starts worshipping God. The compulsions of old age make a woman to become loyal to her husband. In this context, Chanakya says if a man adopts such behaviour without any compulsion, then his importance will be enhanced even more.

Nānnōdakasamaṃ Dānaṃ Na Tithirdvādaśī Samā.
Na Gāyatryā: Parō Mantrō Na Mātu: Paraṃ Daivatam..

17.7 Chanakya says that giving donation is the best thing and most helpful. He considers the donation of food and water to be the most meaningful and fruitful amongst all donations. He says that feeding a hungry person and offering water to a thirsty person is most holistically rewarding. So, as compared to donating wealth, a man should donate food and water more often. Following the religious scriptures, Chanakya also accepts the importance of *dwadashi* (the twelfth day of each half of a lunar month). Likewise, he considers the 'Gayatri Mantra' most superior and the one which fulfills all the desires, amongst all mantras. He says that a man should recite the Gayatri Mantra everyday. It eliminates all the obstructions in life.

Takṣakasya Viṣaṃ Dantē Makṣikāyāstu Mastakē.
Vṛścikasya Viṣaṃ Pucchē Sarvōṅgē Durjanē Viṣam..

17.8 In this shloka, Chanakya has compared an evil person to poisonous animals. He says that like snake, honeybee and scorpion contain poison similarly, an evil person is also filled with deadly poison. The difference being that the snakes poison is in its fangs, honeybee's poison in its forehead and scorpions poison is in its tail; whereas the evil person's entire body is poisonous. Anyone, who comes in his contact, cannot escape from his evil effects. So, a man should stay away from an evil person.

Patyurājñāṃ Vinā Nārī Upōṣya Vratacāriṇī.
Āyuṣyaṃ Haratē Bhartu: Sā Nārī Narakaṃ Vrajēt..

17.9 Chanakya says that obeying the husband and being loyal to him are ornaments of a woman. He says that a woman, who obeys even her husband's minor wishes, her present life and other life, both are reformed. Against this, if she fasts or undertakes religious vows without the permission of her husband, then she can become the cause for his unexpected death. After death, such women have to bear immense torture in hell. So, a woman must obey her husband and be loyal to him these are her duties.

Na Dānai: Śudhyatē Nārī Nōpavāsaśatairapi.
Na Tīrthasēvayā Tadvad Bhartu: Pādōdakairyathā..

17.10 Serving the husband is above all the other auspicious acts. This act has been clarified by Chanakya in this shloka. He says that a loyal woman who is continuously dedicated to serving her husband, need not donate, fast, visit holy shrines or take dip in holy rivers. In fact, being devoted to serving her husband, its self-purifies her.

Dānēna Pāṇirna Tu Kaṅkaṇēna Snānēna aśuddhirna Tu Candanēna.
Mānēna Tṛptirna Tu Bhōjanēna Jñānēna Mukitarna Tu Maṇḍanēna..

17.11 Through this shloka, Chanakya has prompted a man to give up superficial ostentation for self-satisfaction. He says that like the elegance of the hand is not enhanced by wearing jewellery, bangles, etc. but by donation; the body is cleansed by bathing rather than by applying sandalwood paste; mental contentment rests in honour/respect and not in food and salvation is attained by knowledge rather than by applying vermilion or wearing ochercoloured clothes. Just like by superficial ostentation or indulging in sexual lusts, mind does not attain peace or becomes pure. For that inner satisfaction is required, which is only possible by helping others, being kind, being virtuous and with donation.

Nāpitasya Gṛhē Kṣauraṃ Pāṣāṇē Gandhalēpanama.
Ātmarūpaṃ Jalē Paśyan Śakrasyāpi Śriyaṃ Harēt..

17.12 People, who get shaved at the barbers' house, who apply sandalwood paste on stone idols or who see their reflection in the water, Chanakya has called them unwise, inspite of being knowledgeable. According to him, such people ruin their own honour/respect.

Sadya: Prajñāharā Tuṇḍī Sadya: Prajñākarī Vacā.
Sadya: Śakitaharā Nārī Sadya: Śakitakaraṃ Paya:..

17.13 Through this shloka, Chanakya says that like the consumption of Tundi fruit (an intoxicating fruit) destroys wisdom and orris root develops wisdom, likewise a woman robs man's strength and consumption of milk enhances his strength. So, a man should avoid unnecessary and excessive association with a woman.

Parōpakaraṇaṃ Yēṣāṃ Jāgarti Hṛdayē Satām.
Naśyanti Vipadastēṣāṃ Sampada: Syu: Padē Padē..

17.14 According to Chanakya, a man should be filled with the feeling to help others. A man's own welfare lies in helping others. Anyone whose heart is filled with benevolence, never faces crisis. All the obstacles in their path self-destruct and they succeed at every step. Men filled with benevolence do not face sorrows and lead a happy life. So, a man should help others as much as he can.

Yadi Rāmā Yadi Ca Ramā Yadi Tanayō Vinayaguṇōpēta:.
Yadi Tanayē Tanayōatpatti: Suravaranagarē Kimādhikyam..

17.15 Having a pious and loyal wife, having son and daughter-in-law with good qualities and having adequate wealth to meet the needs, Chanakya considers all the three to be important for a man to lead a happy life. He says that if a man gets these three things, then his home will become like heaven and he will have no desire for any other heaven.

Āhāranidrābhayamaiathunāni Samāni Caitāni Nṛṇāṃ Paśūnām.
Jñānaṃ Narāṇāmadhikō Viśēṣō Jñānēna Hīnā: Paśubhi: Samānā:..

17.16 Like all living things in the world, a man also performs activities like eating, sleeping, copulating, producing children and feels fear. From this point of view, apart from the body structure, there is not much difference between man and animals. But only his behaviour makes him superior to animals. In it, true adherence to religion is most important. In fact, anyone who performs religious activities and observes his duties, deserves to be called a human. Anyone bereft of these qualities is like an animal.

Dānārthinō Madhukarā Yadi Karṇatālair
Dūrīkṛtā: Karivarēṇa Madāndhubuddhaya.
Tasyaiva Gaṇḍayugamaṇḍanahānirēṣā
Bhṛṅgā: Punarvikacapadmavanē Vasanti..

17.17 Like the beetles seeking intoxicant from the forehead of a unwise elephant are not bothered by the flapping of its ears to fly them away, they return to the lotus pond. But the elephant loses the grace of its forehead. Similarly, if any evil person chases away a beggar, it makes no difference to the beggar. He gets alms from another house. But the insulted beggar does not go to him again for it would mar his reputation. So, a man should refrain from such tendencies.

Rājā Vēśyā Yamō Hyagnistaskarō Bālayācakau.
Paradu:Khaṃ Na Jānanti Aṣṭamō Grāmakaṇṭaka:..

17.18 King, prostitute, 'Yum' (God of death), fire, smuggler, child, beggar and the villages nuisance creator—these eight do not understand the sorrows and distress of others. Their nature is to act as per their whims. So, a man should not expect any kindness from them.

Adha: Paśyasi Kiṃ Bālē Patitaṃ Tava Kiṃ Bhuvi.
Rē Rē Mūrkha Na Jānāsi Gataṃ Tāruṇyamaukitakam..

17.19 A man should never mock any helpless and afflicted person, because tomorrow he may also be in the same situation. Chanakya has clarified it further in this shloka. An impertinent boy laughing, asked an old woman "Oh young girl! What are you searching?" Hearing his mocking tone, the old woman said, "Due to my old age, my youth in the *avatar* of a pearl has fallen down, I am searching it." In this context, Chanakya says that sooner or later, a man has to definitely face old age. So, a man should refrain from the tendency to mock others.

Vyālāśrayāpa Viphalāpi Sakaṇṭakāpa
Vakrāpi Paṅkila Bhavāpi Durāsadāpi.
Gandhēna Bandhurasi Kētaki Sarvajantōra
Ēkō Guṇa: Khalu Nihanti Samastadōṣān..

17.20 Sometimes, even one good quality overrides many bad qualities. Because of only one good quality, inspite of having several bad qualities, a man earns honour/respect in the society. In this context, Chanakya gives the example of 'Ketki tree' (source of kewra essence—extract of pandanus flower). He says that snakes habituate on the Ketki tree. It is crooked and grows in slime but its fragrance bewitches everyone. This one good quality covers all other bad qualities. Similarly, even if a man keeps company of evil persons, is ugly looking, is born in low caste but is wise and intelligent, inspite of having many bad qualities, he is respected in the gathering of scholars.

❑